LOVE SKULL

Emma Alice Johnson

WEIRD

PUNK

CONTENTS

ANIMAL BEHAVIOR

I WAS FAR LESS SHOCKED BY THE APPEARANCE OF A PREVIOUSLY unknown forty-foot tall animal crashing through the city than I was by the city's approach to dealing with it, which was to lure it to an abandoned warehouse and blow it up.

I stood atop city hall next to the mayor, the police chief and several others. I wanted to carefully observe the animal and note aggressive behaviors that could prove valuable in understanding it. Only a couple blocks away, it scaled the warehouse, making its way to the top, where a half-dozen Holsteins awaited.

My observation was interrupted when the mayor grabbed my hand like a child and dragged me behind a wall of sandbags. The warehouse exploded and the sky filled with fire and brick and burning livestock. I shook free of the mayor's grip and poked my head up from behind the barricade. The animal's yellow eyes pierced the clearing smoke. I realized I was directly in its line of sight and felt a fear I had never experienced in the field, or anywhere else: Not when that desert warthog nearly took my fingers off in Kenya thinking I was one of the poachers who hurt her, nor when a pack of spider monkeys swarmed me in Ecuador. Not even close.

Enough of the smoke dissipated to allow a ray of light to gleam on the animal's purple-gray exoskeleton. Smoke puffed from the animal's massive, twitching nostrils. The heat had likely burned down the animal's nasal passage, wreaking havoc in its lungs. I could almost feel its anger.

The screams of citizens now rose above the din of the settling debris. The streets had been cleared in preparation, but many had gathered around city hall, balloons in hand, in hopes of being the first to celebrate the demise of the animal that had terrorized their streets. They fled as the unfazed animal crawled toward them, toward me.

Close now, the animal reared up. Shriveled crimson wings fanned out from its rutty back, flapping them to drive away the last of the smoke, creating a wind so powerful I could feel the debris against my face, forcing me to squint to protect my eyes from dust. It rounded its layers of lips, baring jagged teeth. Its proboscis stretched out from inside its salivating maw, flicking the air as it moved closer.

I stumbled backward and fell on my ass, wondering between my cacophonous heartbeats whether this would be my last day, and what about my lost future I should mourn in the moments of life that remained.

Then the animal simply turned away, quietly leaving the way it had come.

The mayor and the police chief fumed at the failure. The mayor threw his cellphone off the roof while the chief yelled into his walkie-talkie. I stood, dusted myself off and composed myself. Then I snapped my fingers in front of the mayor's face to draw him out of his fit.

"Where does it go?" I asked, trying to hold on tight to the quickly fading excitement that had driven me, against the advice of my colleagues, to choose this opportunity over a fully funded study of polar bears near the Hudson Bay.

He looked at me dumbfounded.

I asked again, "When it leaves here, where does it go?"

He huffed and raised his voice over the sound of the sirens as fire trucks circled the charred remains of the warehouse and firefighters began to quell the flames. "The hills, probably. Or maybe it flies somewhere."

"Its wings didn't look functional," I replied. "Possibly vestigial."

"Vestigial?"

"Like an ostrich's."

The mayor crossed his arms and glared at me. "You're the animal lady that Deb called in?"

"I prefer ethologist to animal lady, but yes." I held out my hand. "Dr. Violet Purpose."

The mayor took my hand and squeezed it too hard, then held it for a moment as if waiting for me to squeeze back harder. I pulled away, refusing to partake in his ritual of machismo. "Hank," he said. "Sorry, I'm a bit frazzled, Doctor. I really thought that would do the trick. Any idea how it could have survived that?"

"It appears to have an exoskeleton, which is not only unprecedented, but biomechanically untenable per the square cube law. In theory, all of its guts should be a pile of mush at the very bottom of its shell, but it seems to be doing fine. Regardless, the exoskeleton would have to be quite strong for an animal that size. That being said, my specialty is animal behavior, not biology."

The mayor nodded.

"Also, and I'm no explosives expert, but it looks like the explosion may have been engineered to destroy the building itself, rather than the surrounding area."

"Well, obviously."

"But the animal was in the surrounding area, not inside the building."

The mayor squinted into the cloud of smoke swirling out

of the burning warehouse. "Yeah, I suppose it was. Should we have waited until it was on the roof, do you think?" Without waiting for an answer, he shouted at the police chief, who was still distracted by his walkie talkie, huddled behind the sandbags, "You should have waited until it was on the roof, Todd!"

THE ANIMAL HAD KILLED 26 people before the city thought to bring me in. They had "tried everything" to get it to stop. Of course, to them, "everything" meant attempting to poison it, shoot it and now blow it up. I was only here as an afterthought at the behest of Deb, the mayor's daughter, who ran the local zoo.

She had seen a YouTube video of my talk about differences in aggressive behavior in true lobsters versus those in false lobsters, bringing the video's number of views to 2. She reached out to me via email. Her note was elusive and strangely complimented my pricy purple blazer and pencil skirt as being "not what I expected from a lesbian animal professional." By then I had heard news of the city's troubles, however, so I easily ascertained what she was proposing.

As I described in the video, and I assume Deb understood, was if one understands why an animal is acting aggressively, and can pinpoint the stimuli causing the aggressive behavior, then one may be able to curtail the aggressive acts. However, it's not as easy as saying that rodeo bulls charge on the sight of red, so let's not show them that color. They don't, so hiding it won't stop them. There's biology and psychology, neither of which take place in a vacuum. This animal's aggressive behavior may not have even been typical for its species. In fact, it probably wasn't, or we would have seen others before. More likely, something happened to this one that prompted it to lash out, and it was very specifically lashing out at the city of Carringhouse.

Regardless, there I was, picking debris out of my blonde curls as I followed the mayor and the others back inside, where he directed me to an empty cubicle and said, "Good luck!" Baffled, I sat down and watched these men walk away. Then I turned to the desk, empty but for a dusty, out-of-date computer, and wondered if they simply expected me to science up some solutions for them.

I opened the drawers one at a time and found a calculator from 1985 and a crinkled piece of paper with typing on it. No words, just globs of inky letters, as if whoever had done the typing thought they might be able to fix the machine by banging on the keys. I had done the same thing at age eight, when my parents had thrifted me a typewriter so I could write "scientific reports," as I called them, about the grasshoppers I found in the yard.

I spun around a few times in the office chair, considering whether it was too late for me to beg my way back onto the polar bear project. The bear people really wanted me. I had done a grizzly bear study and they likely thought bears were bears, which, in all honesty, wasn't super wrong, but I probably wouldn't say that to someone paying me, or to any of my peers either, as they would likely snark that I had spent too much time with lobsters. Which I had. The polar bear project was more about mating though, which was only tangentially related to my specialty – animal aggression. Well, maybe more than tangentially related.

I sent a terse email to Deb. Then I found the bathroom, wiped the thick layer of soot off my face, and tracked down the mayor in his office.

He stood up eagerly. "Do you have something? Already?"

I studied his earnest face, his powder blue eyes, the deep wrinkles that seemed almost to drip out of his skin. "No."

He sat back down.

"Typically, when I arrive at a project, I'm provided with, well, anything?"

He looked at me sincerely, almost apologetically. "Doctor, I read about you before I gave Deb the okay to bring you in. I realize you're the top of your field and well respected at whatever that institute is in Vienna. I appreciate that you came here.

"Carrington is a small city, with hills on one side and desert on the other. We have 30,000 people in the city proper, and a bunch more out in the hills. They're good people, easygoing. It doesn't take much to keep the place running – me and the chief and the fire chief and the council ladies and the school board. Deb runs the zoo, but one of the exhibits is a bunch of kittens. You go there and just sit with the kittens. There are 20 kittens in our zoo and a three-legged mountain lion. That's our city, okay? Honestly, my secretary does a heck of a lot and she's on pregnancy leave.

"You're the first scientist I've spoken to in my life. I don't know what you need. I don't know what ethology is, really. I don't know what to do. I just know I need to fix this, and would love your help."

"I need as much information as possible," I told him, softly, as it looked like he might cry if I pushed too hard. "Any pictures or videos of the animal, any information about the timing of the attacks, commonalities between the victims and the victims' actions leading up to the attacks, details about the animal's actions prior to the attacks – anything that might reveal a pattern, help me understand the animal's cognition or, better yet, provide a clue as to how to get it to disengage from this behavior."

The mayor nodded. "The chief is good at paperwork. He'll have detailed reports. But let me ask you…" He paused, as if wondering if he should go through with the question now that he had introduced it. "What would you call it?"

"I think it's safe to say it's an unknown species," I replied.
"Yes, yes, so what should we call it?"

ON MY WAY out of city hall, I bumped into Deb. She hugged me awkwardly around my arms so tightly I couldn't reciprocate.

"I am glad you're here. You are so inspiring. I've loved animals since I was a little girl, but until I saw your videos I never really got how complex they are and how little we truly understand about them and, oh gosh, you are just beautiful."

Small town lesbians can be so weird. Back in Chicago, I can't throw a rock without hitting a queer, so I take for granted that we aren't everywhere. I suspected that Carringhouse wasn't filled with educated gays, so I was probably something pretty special to this woman.

I withdrew from her overeager hug and took her in. She wasn't not my type. A bit young, and less put together than most of the ladies I dated, but thick and sincere – qualities I gravitated toward. "Thank you. Sorry for my terse email."

"I told them to give you everything they had. I really did. These guys, they just… These men have good hearts and they run this city with those hearts, but the most drama my dad has faced in the last twenty years on the job was the debate about expanding the school so it could accommodate the hill kids."

I bit my tongue to prevent making a potentially rude comment about the frequency of excuses I'd already heard and their correlation with the nowhere-close-to-being-resolved animal issue. "Can you drive me to the police station?"

"Of course."

As she drove, I surveyed the damage to the city. When I

was doing the Alaska grizzly study, I read about a case of a bear that would come into a village. It killed several pets and one drunken teenager. In the process, it smashed a bus stop, tore down a door, that sort of thing. The damage was incidental. It hadn't just torn up structures for the sake of it, only what was in its way. This looked similar.

An animal the size of the one terrorizing Carringhouse could have easily done much more damage if its intent had been to smash the place. Instead, it toppled a couple houses and crushed some cars parked on the street. When I have so little evidence, I typically don't introduce theories. But the reality is that aberrant aggressive animal behavior often comes down to food, as in the bear situation.. Like the bear, this animal likely wasn't getting its food needs met in its traditional hunting area, so it was forced to venture into new territory for the sake of its own survival. In a sense, the city was already aware of that, as it had lured it in with Holsteins to eat.

"How many times has the animal appeared?" I asked.

I realized Deb had been staring at me.

"And what was the frequency of the appearances?" I added, hoping I could pile on enough questions to prevent her from working her way around to what I knew she was thinking about saying, which would in turn force me to decide how to respond to what I knew she was thinking about saying.

"I'm gay too," she said.

"Yes, I had ascertained that."

"Did you? I don't really act gay though. This is still one of those places. Like, we voted for that president, you know? There's a gay bar, but it's bears and drag queens and I just feel out of place. Everyone's nice, but the only women who come in are straight girls who watch Drag Race or whatever."

Part of me really wanted to have a discussion with her about the concept of "acting gay" and what was packed into that statement, but I figured I'd have better luck tackling the giant animal conundrum than I would trying to parse out this woman's internalized heterosexism. And anyway, I was not in any position to play the role of queery godmother swooping in to teach the young, small town lesbo the ways of the gays. I hadn't had sex in two years, and that had been with my ex's current girlfriend, which had cost me most of my friend group and my goldfish.

"It… it… ummm, it gets better." I cringed at how disingenuous I sounded.

She laughed, a pretty, expressive laugh that somehow landed her hand on my thigh. When she calmed down, she said, "I think you're really something."

My cheeks heated up and I knew they were turning red.

This was how it happened. This was how I stumbled into relationships. Some gorgeous girl just laid claim to me and I swooned, in love with the confidence it took to do such a thing as much as I was in love with the woman doing the thing, which every coiled bit of my brain realized was not the foundation of a great relationship, but that my thump-thumping heart always thought was worth a shot.

Not this time, though. I had a plan that involved meeting another professional, established in her field, my age or older. I had invested in this plan, and I was not going to give up on that investment for a random zookeeper with warm hands.

"How old are you?" I asked, shifting so that her hand slid off my thigh, leaving it cold where her palm had been.

"I'm eighteen."

"Oh!" I said, shocked. "I assumed you were older because you run the zoo."

"You need to be old to run a zoo? No, I opened that zoo when I was twelve, which was before my dad became mayor. Everyone thinks I got the zoo because my dad became mayor, but that's not even true. Wait, I'll show it to you!"

"I really should focus on the giant animal destroying your town."

"Focus on it at the zoo. Trust me, this will help."

Recognizing that I would not be able to change this woman's mind, we stopped at the police station and she wouldn't let me get out of the car. She ran in and reappeared minutes later with a box of documents – hard copies, of course – which she slid into the backseat. "The chief is good at paperwork."

AT THE ZOO, she parked, got out of the car and ran around to my side. She opened my door and held out her hand to help me out, which nobody had done for me since Dave Oscrack took me out to Denny's when I was 16. I took her hand, and her skin against mine unleashed all the romantic fantasies I had locked away after Dave had stuck me with the check when I asked him what he thought about boys who liked other boys and girls who liked other girls.

Thankfully, there was an undescribed forty-foot animal to worry about instead of imagining me and Deb curled up on my couch reading books and listening to indie rock. I needed to resolve that and then I was going to fly out of this town all by myself. I was not going to take anyone's heart with me, nor leave mine behind.

I smiled tersely and tried to tell her as much with my eyes, but I think I did it wrong, because she just smiled back and held onto my hand well after I was out of the car and standing securely on the sidewalk in front of her zoo.

"It's two city blocks," she said with pride, reluctantly dropping my hand so she could retrieve the document box from the backseat.

I had been to my fair share of zoos, though not as many

as some suspected considering my occupation, but I had never seen anything like this. A series of four cages and three sheds adorned a field of dirt. In the far corner stood a main building that looked like the restrooms found at parks. I approached the closest cage and scanned the trees within to see what hid inside. It didn't take long. The pair of albino squirrels didn't camouflage well against the dust and dying foliage.

"We had a contest to name them and a 5-year old girl won. So they're both named Chad." Deb shrugged. "We call them the Chads."

"Chadtastic," I said, groaning at my own bad joke, which was made worse by Deb's sincere giggle. I did not need to hear that giggle. I reminded myself that I was here because people had died and my role was to provide insight that might be able to prevent more from dying. I needed to be giggle-impenetrable.

I followed Deb on the walking path, past a picnic area where an elderly couple ate fried chicken and laughed. She led me to the main building. I opened the door for her since she had the box in her hands, and she smiled at the gesture even though I had thought it more practical than romantic. When the door clicked shut behind me, I was swarmed. Kittens of all shapes and sizes poked at my feet, scrambled up my shins, meowed furiously. Without thinking, I scooped up a chubby orange purr monster and held her tight to my chest.

"We're up to 30 kittens. As you can see, we've also got beds, couches and chairs. People can come and cuddle and just be filled with warmth. And they do. On Saturdays we're lucky if each guest gets one kitten. Sometimes the kittens will like one guest more than another, and they'll attack her while leaving another guest alone. I try to balance it out, but kittens do what they want to do. They like you!"

I nodded. I had never been a cat lady. Not that I didn't like them. They are wonderful creatures. But they are wonderful creatures whose litter boxes needed to be emptied and whose hair and grime got everywhere, and who insisted on eating any piece of plastic they could find and puking it up.

"It's certainly a unique idea," I said.

"Word of mouth is getting out too. We have people come from out of state just for this. If I had the time to promote it, we could probably become a big tourist attraction, but we prefer it being our little secret."

I put the cat down. A little black one tried to jump into my arms in its place, but I shooed it away and crossed my arms across my chest. "Are you worried that the animal will attack here? The fact that it went after the livestock makes me think that its strikes are motivated by hunger."

Deb dropped the box onto a big, cushy couch and kittens immediately began scratching the cardboard. She futilely tried to push them away. "Oh, what's it gonna eat here? The biggest we have is the cougar, Benjamin."

"Benjamin? Another naming contest?"

"No, I named him. He looks like a Benjamin." She sat beside the box and patted the seat next to her, gesturing for me to sit. "Shall we dig in?"

I nodded and sat. As kittens filled my lap, Deb filled my hands with papers. The first was a police report with "First Attack" written in red on the upper corner. The animal had snatched a teenager up near the edge of the city while his mother watched. A picture of a severed hand was affixed to the report. A tabby batted at the picture with its paw, meowing louder and louder.

Deb scooted closer to me.

Feeling her eyes on me, I asked, "What do you hypothesize?"

"Well, I think we know it's coming in for food, right?" A cat climbed onto Deb's shoulder. "Looking at these reports, it's clear that every time it has come in, it has eaten one or two or three people and left. I think that was proven by it going straight for the Holsteins. But I'm not sure how this knowledge helps?"

"It helps us prevent it from eating people, for one. We know it wants food, so we give it food. Are there any patterns in terms of the frequency of attacks?"

Deb shuffled through the papers. "Every 10 days, roughly. But it's not like we've got some endless supply of livestock we can set out for it."

"No, that would be a temporary solution. The real work will be determining what prompted it to start coming here and remedy that issue."

"Or we could just kill it."

"Or you could just kill it. Though it seems you have tried that."

"We'll leave that for the men to figure out."

I laughed at that, despite my distaste for stereotyping, and she laughed too. She played her thumb under the strap of her cami. I moved away from her, but accidentally sat on a cat's tail. It yowled, but forgave me when I pet it behind the ears. While I was distracted, Deb snuck in closer, pressing her thigh against mine.

"You're super pretty," she said.

"Listen, you're very…"

She interrupted me. "Don't you dare!"

Taken aback, I looked away, unable to take the double stare of her and the tabby on her shoulder. They both seemed really angry. "What?"

"Don't you dare play wise old lesbian who martyrs her own desire to her magnanimity because she doesn't want to break the poor naïve girl's heart."

"What?" I repeated. I shoveled cats off my lap and stood. Reaching for the box, I said, "I really should go back to my motel and get to work. And I need a shower anyway. Look at me, I'm filthy from the explosion."

"Yeah, whatever."

"How dare you bring me here under false pretenses!" I yelled, taking my turn at being angry, as one of the kittens jumped into the box of papers before I could pick it up. "I am one of the most renowned ethologists in North America."

"Oh, listen to you."

I lifted the kitten out of the box and put her down on the couch where I had been sitting. "Did you think I was just going to come here and fall in love with you?"

"I thought you were going to come here and fuck me."

"Why? Why would you think that? Because you complimented my outfits?" Two different kittens hopped into the box and began kicking each other playfully.

"I guess I made a mistake. I guess I read you as being smart and sex-positive, not some old prude, but obviously I was wrong."

I took a kitten in each hand to remove them from the box, but another one jumped in and started scratching the cardboard. I shouted, "This is ridiculous."

Deb grinned at me.

I rolled my eyes and stomped toward the door.

"You can't take those," Deb said to my back, giggling that giggle.

I glanced down to see that I still held the two kittens. On the couch, the box now teemed with cats, as if it had been filled with catnip. I bent over to put the cats down and another one jumped onto my back. Slowly, I moved into a standing position, but the kitten moved up onto my shoulder, and then onto my head.

"They're not going to let you leave."

I sighed, carefully untangling the cat's paws from my curls. "I see that."

"Do you really want to leave?"

I pulled the cat to my chest and felt its warmth. Its purring resonated through my sternum. A black kitten with white paws rolled upside down on my foot as it tried to undo my shoelaces. In front of me, a gorgeous young lady smiled at me sincerely, holding a box of documents that could let me unravel a mystery that no one in my field or any other field had ever heard of before.

"No," I said. "No, I don't."

FIVE WAYS TO KILL YOUR
RAPIST ON A FARM

THE FIRST TIME SHE KILLED HER RAPIST, SHE USED A HAY BALE hook.

Her rapist's arrival interrupted her as she sternly lectured a woodchuck that hid in the cracked foundation of the danger barn. She called it the danger barn because it had partially collapsed and looked like it could topple at any moment. Shards of glass littered the floor. Coils of rusty barbed wire dangled from the support beams. A woodchuck glowered at her from the concrete.

On summer Sundays like these, she enjoyed following critters as they went on their little errands. This one's errands had involved chewing up the bottom of her car, so she'd chased it to its current hiding spot to admonish it about respecting other people's property.

The sound of tires on her gravel driveway forced her to stop before she was certain the furball understood. She didn't know the car belonged to her rapist, not at first. Most days, she got to exist free of interactions with other humans, and she preferred it that way. Not that she was antisocial. She was plenty social, mostly with bumblebees and wildflowers. Occasionally, a delivery person came with a package, or some teenagers pulled in to beg to hunt on her land, and she'd chat with them.

She peeked out of the danger barn. A car with Minneapolis plates parked by the house. She didn't recognize it as belonging to one of her friends from back home, and people from the cities usually didn't stray so far into Wisconsin. Her immediate instinct was, it's him, it's the man who raped me.

She chastised herself for thinking this. She'd spent the last couple of years training herself to shove such thoughts aside. In the days following the sexual assault, she'd seen his face on every man she passed. She'd broken down screaming at the grocery store when she turned into an aisle and saw him, fled her doctor's office because he sat in the clinic's waiting room. Her therapist had assured her that this was normal, her brain stuck on survival mode.

It had never been him on those occasions, and surely it wasn't him now. It had been more than two years. The trial long over, he'd been convicted, put on probation, and gotten on with his life. The restraining order was still active. And how would he even know where she lived? Only a few of her friends had her address. She'd moved far from the city to make sure she never saw him again.

But when the car door opened, her rapist got out. She panicked, ducked back into the danger barn, glanced at the crack in the concrete where the groundhog hid, and wished she could join. Why would he come here?

After the trial, his friends had taken to social media to convince people that he'd been the victim of a travesty of justice, that she'd made a mistake, misremembered. He even did a fundraiser to pay his mortgage because he lost his job. A big boo-hoo that so many people fell for. Even with her word, even with all the evidence, even with a jury convicting him of felony sexual assault, so many people refused to believe a woman. Maybe he'd come to kill her, to finish what he'd started. If everyone refused to believe he was a rapist, maybe they'd refuse to believe he was a murderer too.

From in the barn, she heard him knocking on the front door of her house. She considered waiting him out, hiding here until he left. For a moment, that plan seemed reasonable, until she realized that if he had found her now, he could find her later, tonight, anytime. She'd never not be thinking about when he'd come back. That's when she picked up the bale hook.

When she bought the farm, she'd had so much fun digging through everything the previous owner, and each owner before that, had left behind. Some of the tools she found had likely been here since the house was first built in 1893. Jagged, bladed things, dinged from years of use and oranged with rust. The bale hook had immediately piqued her curiosity. A half-foot long metal hook attached to a U-shaped piece of metal, with a handle running across its prongs. Not being from a farming background, she hadn't known what it was. At first, she thought it was a meat hook. Meat hooks were usually S-shaped though, one side to impale the meat on, and the other side to hang it. A neighbor corrected her, told her that farmers used the bale hook to grab bales of hay, pull them off a trailer and toss them into the barn.

She gave the shush finger to the woodchuck, who wedged deeper into the crack. She liked the way the tool felt in her hand, light, natural. She kept a loose grip as she emerged from the danger barn. She rarely wore shoes unless she was going deep into the woods, so her bare feet made little noise as she stepped through the lush green grass toward the house.

Her rapist stood facing the door, knocking occasionally. How very city of him to come to this farm in the woods, on a day when the sun kissed the world to life, and assume she was sitting inside. In moments, she was behind him. He didn't notice. She stood there for a beat, enough to take a deep breath. Then she swung the hook and sunk the blade into the side of his neck, right below the spot where his jawbone met his ear.

Before he could turn around, she pulled, using both hands now, dragging him off his feet. She yanked again. He flailed at the tool as it dug deeper into his neck. She thought about farmers sticking the hooks into bales of hay and wondered, once they had moved the bale where they wanted it, how did they get the hook free? She tried wiggling it. Eventually it came loose. He didn't put up much of a fight, just pushed awkwardly at the hole and grunted. Blood spurted from between his fingers.

Standing above him, she wasn't certain she'd done enough to kill him. She wanted to, she realized. She'd wanted to since that night, since she'd woken up to his weight on top of her, to her dress pushed up and tights pulled down.

She kneeled beside him and drove the bloody bale hook into his ear, but couldn't get it in very far. He slapped at her now, writhed and kicked, flopped around on the grass. She lost her grip on the tool for a second.

When she got hold of it again, she sat on her bottom. She straightened her legs and pressed her heels against the side of his face opposite the ear she had hooked. Pushing his head away from her with her feet and pulling the bale hook toward her with her arms, she drove the hook in deeper and deeper. She strained her hamstrings.

When she thought she couldn't do anymore, she gripped the tool's handle even harder and stomped her feet against his head, impaling him further onto the hook. He soon stopped moving. When she had pulled so hard her forearms felt likely to combust, she released her grip and lay flat on her back. She thrashed out with her feet, driving the body away from her.

A sound under her car drew her attention, teeth on metal. She glanced over and saw the woodchuck, gnawing at some wires dangling from the vehicle's undercarriage. The critter looked at her. She held her pointer finger to her lips, shushing.

THE SECOND TIME she killed her rapist was the cutest.

Can you even imagine the sort of hunger pigs must feel, after humans have spent centuries breeding them into insatiable eating machines so they will grow as big as possible as quickly as possible? She thinks about that a lot when she feeds her four pigs. When dinner time comes, they thrash and roar in anticipation. How they must ache. How hollow they must feel inside. But then she feeds them buttered potatoes and their eyes gleam at her with such sweet gratitude.

She fed them much more than buttered potatoes today. She'd spotted her rapist on her way back from the feed store. He was changing his tire on the shoulder of 64. Different car this time, but definitely him, and obviously on the way to her place. She hadn't thought about it, just the gentlest little nudge of the steering wheel and she grazed him with the side of her car, enough to knock him out, bloody him up and make it easy to drag him into her backseat.

At first, the pigs wouldn't eat him. They were used to pellets, plus the odd fruit or veggie. The only time they'd eaten meat was when she'd found one of her chickens with its head ripped off and fed them the remains. Maybe this body seemed too much like her, so they didn't want to eat it. That thought disgusted her, because she was nothing like him. She understood how her pigs might make the mistake though, even though he was tied up, lying in the slop with his mouth taped shut. Or maybe his contortions threw them off.

She ran into the house and scoured her cupboards until she found just the thing. Back out in the pen, she smeared a handful of peanut butter on his face, used her pointer finger to get nice globs of it in his nostrils and ears. His incessant blinking made it hard for her to pack it around his eyes. Before she could, the pigs started digging in. His body went still pretty soon after that.

Her oldest pig, a 400-pound Yorkshire sow, pulled away, crunching on a chunk of her rapist's skull. Excited, the pig spun in circles so fast it fell down into the slop beside the body. The other three pigs, still gilts, barely 200 pounds, were more focused. They rooted into the bowl of red mush her rapist's face had become, slurping, their coiled tails whirling with joy. She'd watched those pigs use their snouts to flip cinderblocks like they were nothing in order to get at the centipedes and other bugs hiding underneath. Human bones were no obstacle for them.

As the pigs ate, they pushed the man's head so he looked like he was nodding, the same way he'd nodded while she testified against him, as if agreeing with everything she said. She'd wanted to stand up and scream, "Why are you nodding? Why are you making me go through this if you know what I'm saying is true?" But then he'd taken the stand and told the jury that she'd remembered wrong, that she'd consented, and that she'd been awake the whole time.

For a moment, she worried the pigs would only eat the head and leave the rest for her to deal with. To entice them, she smeared peanut butter on her rapist's fingers and toes. She noticed he didn't have tattoos anymore. Maybe he'd gotten them removed. Could tattoos be removed so quickly?

Before she could finish with the peanut butter, the sow got back to business. She was surprised to see her rapist pull his hand away. Was it a mere death twitch, or was he still alive in there? One of the gilts looked up at her, a piece of the man's brain hanging from its dazzlingly long chin whiskers, so she figured it was unlikely that he was still living.

Every once in a while, the pigs pulled their mouth away from their meal, lifted their heads to the sky and smiled, oinking their celebratory oinks. "I love you, my sweet girls," she said, petting their muscley pink rumps and booping their blood-soaked snoots. Just the cutest thing in the whole world.

THE THIRD TIME she killed her rapist, she tried stoning him. This was a mistake. Do not try to kill your rapist by throwing rocks at him.

She caught him hiking in the woods near her farm, his skinny body all decked out with a backpack and a shiny canteen. When they crossed paths, he acted as though he was lost, as if he hadn't come to hurt her again. She knew the truth though. She picked up a stone and hurled it at him. It thunked on his shoulder, which didn't damage him so much as anger him.

She bolted, weaving through the trees. She'd walked these woods every day since she moved here, so she knew her way around. Keeping a steady pace, she did her best not to lose him without giving him the idea that she was leading him somewhere. Which, of course, she was.

She cut across her neighbor's cornfield to the old silo on the edge of her property. A sturdy tube of concrete, walls at least a foot thick. It hadn't been used in decades. Inside, the bottom dropped out, a twenty-foot fall to a pool of stagnant water. Mosquitos swarmed the entrance. She ignored them and ducked inside. There, next to the entrance, a steel ladder was built into the wall. It went up, but not down. She clung to it, waiting for her rapist to follow her.

As expected, the man stuck his head inside the door, cursing at her about the thrown rock. With her feet firmly on the bottom rung of the ladder and one hand gripping another, she used her free hand to snatch the man's collar. With a quick pull, she flung him into the water below. He splashed toward the wall, screaming, slapping at the concrete as if he could scrabble up it.

She thought about how, upon waking up to find him on top of her, she'd kicked away from him, crawled backwards from that couch. All the while, he'd just stood there in the shadows, watching as she screamed, savoring her panic, as if this was the moment he had been waiting for, not the act itself. He'd lost weight since then, she noticed. A lot of weight. He seemed younger too. Not fair. She'd aged a decade in the two years since he raped her.

She swung herself out of the silo and grabbed one of the cinderblocks stacked outside the entrance. This time, her aim was true. The block fell onto the man's bald head, collapsing it. Almost instantaneously, he and the block disappeared beneath the surface, leaving a little dab of red to delight the skeeters.

THE FOURTH TIME she killed her rapist, she got creative.

She enjoyed tinkering with the old machines she found in the barn, the smaller ones at least, or the larger ones she could figure out how to disassemble. Not that she was mechanically inclined. She didn't know what half of them were, but most had a screw or a bolt somewhere that she could undo, and the next thing she knew, she'd have a bunch of rusty metal parts spread out in front of her in the grass. She'd clean them, maybe oil them, and put them back together, replacing any screws or bolts that broke. She'd been proud when she got an old weed whipper to work again that way, and she'd gotten a kick out of cutting down tall grass as the machine roared. It felt powerful.

Her rapist began popping up again, driving by, pretending to be the mailman. Naturally, the idea crossed her mind to use the weed whipper on him. But she didn't think the orange string could do as much damage to him as she'd require. It had been foiled by a few saplings she'd tried to cut down, so it didn't stand much of a chance against bone.

She loved the concept though, of whipping him down to bits, so she started tinkering. The first thing she tried was attaching a chain to the head of the weed whipper. A chain would definitely do the trick, and she found a big one in the danger barn. She duct-taped it onto the head of the weed whipper, but the tape got gummed in the works, and the machine wasn't powerful enough to spin the weight of the chain.

After a lot of daydreaming, she decided to dissect her riding lawnmower. She excavated the spinning parts out of the housing, inverted them, punched holes in the blades, and threaded the chains through. She mounted it on a wagon, along with the engine and battery. It didn't exactly work like a charm. She had to hopscotch away fast after she started it, to get clear of the chain before it picked up momentum. For a brief moment, it spun perfectly, before it worked itself into a frenzy, tipped over, and whipped up a cloud of dirt until it choked to a stop. Good enough, she thought.

The next day, she wheeled her little death robot out and hid with it behind some brush on the side of the street opposite her mailbox. As she waited, she thought about how, in court, her rapist's lawyer had asked her how many times she'd kissed him before she passed out. How many kisses, she wondered, would have made what that man did to her okay?

When her rapist came by, she waited till he reached out to open her mailbox and shove some letters in, then she started the death robot and kicked it out at his car. One of the wagon's wheels flopped off along the way. The machine leapt and sparked on the blacktop, throwing an epic hissy fit. In the process, it managed to smash her rapist's side mirror before sputtering out with a loud *chunka chunka chunka* noise.

Not what she had hoped for, but it distracted her rapist enough that she was able to open his door and smash his face with a hammer before he could even take his eyes off the smoking machine.

THE FIFTH AND final time she killed her rapist was a real barn burner.

He hung limp from a ceiling joist in the danger barn, wrapped snuggly in rusted barbed wire. She'd been careful not to get any of the wire around his neck, not wanting him to strangle. Instead, she wrapped it under his arms. She also coiled some around his face, piercing one of his eyes in the process. That's when he passed out, his cornea gobbed up on the barb as she pulled the wire taut and snipped off the excess. That had made it easy for her to hoist him up to where he hung.

Now, she stood near the inside wall of the barn, peering through a crack to see her house, where a group of police officers gathered at the door, knocking. They'd been there a minute already. Soon enough, they'd give up and start snooping around the outbuildings, and the danger barn was the closest to the house. She'd have to move quickly.

She splashed gasoline on her rapist. He bled pretty bad now from all his puncture wounds. The blood trailed down his body, disappeared into his shoes, and dripped from the toes, where it had soaked through. His body quivered as he wormed his way back into consciousness.

"You look different," she told him. He was missing the thumb and pinky on his left hand. She wondered when that had happened. Her neighbor at the adjacent farm had a similar layout, she remembered. He'd told her he'd gotten messy with his dad's circular saw as a teen. Maybe her rapist had tried to hurt someone else, and they'd gotten at him with a saw. Well, there'd be no more of that, thanks to her.

She lit a match and flicked it at him. He caught fire fast. He fully regained consciousness in time to scream as his face melted off his skull.

She'd been sloppy with the gas, and soon the whole barn was aflame. The police came running, but stood a safe distance outside the entrance, staring in at her. She saw that they weren't police at all. Each one was her rapist, costumed in black, even outfitted with a badge and a gun. She couldn't believe the lengths he'd go to so he could keep hurting her.

"Come out, now!" they shouted.

They raised their guns at her. As the air heated up, she thought the threat funny. Did they intend to shoot her if she didn't come out? Would they fill her with bullets before she could catch fire? They couldn't stand to give up control of her.

She turned back to her rapist, the one suspended inside her burning barn. The fire had no itinerary, no rhyme or reason. In some spots, it burned through to her rapist's bones, while patches of his shirt collar and underwear still remained. His legs had blackened and looked bizarrely thin as the meat dissolved from them. Fluid leaked from tiny fissures in one femur, fizzling and popping.

Flaming hunks of rafters fell around her and a spark caught her hair on fire. She braced herself for pain, feeling an odd sense of ease knowing that at least he wouldn't be able to come after her anymore. Gazing out at the men standing outside her barn with guns pointed, she wished she could burn them too. She wished she could burn every last one of them.

NECKSNAPPER

DELAYNA SNAPPED THE FIRST CROW'S NECK WITHOUT THINKING about it. She had learned this from her parents. Not the act itself, but the ability to do such things without letting them weigh on her. Before they robbed and prostituted their way out of her life and into prison, they had taught her to ignore the weight of sin and instead focus on doing what needed to be done to get by. Their lessons, though masterful, hadn't completely taken. The weight of what she had done in the past had been too much for her. This though, this dead bird in her hand, it didn't weigh much at all.

Reaching out from behind the camera, the director snatched the black-feathered corpse from Delayna and flung it onto the concrete floor of the Burbank warehouse. "One down, nine-hundred and ninety-nine to go," he said.

The director's aged hands did constant battle with the white hair that stuck to his ever-shiny forehead. Watching the old man made Delayna feel inadequate about her lack of primping. She combed her short blonde shocks in the morning and let them do whatever they wanted during the day—no tending. By nighttime, they stuck out at odd angles like straw from holes in a worn-out scarecrow.

She had made contact with the director via a website where she often found video work. The work was dicey, but far from the path her parents had taken. Mostly on the right side of the law or only a couple steps over. She didn't have the looks for traditional porn—chin too wide, forehead too short —but she had the guts for the out-there stuff, the whips-and-chains stuff, the oozes-and-eels stuff. This was a first though.

Upon meeting the director, her first question had been, "Won't the crows fly away?" The old man had laughed and explained the assembly line setup: one man would take a crow from the massive cage and hand it to the anesthetist, who would inject it and hold it tight until the drugs kicked in. The anesthetist would then give it to the director, who would turn it over to Delayna.

Now, the assembly line shifted into gear. Another crow appeared in Delayna's hands. Alive, but barely. It had been injected with enough tranquilizers to prevent it from flying away, but not enough to stop it from desperately flapping its wings and chomping its beak.

When she snapped the crow's neck, she didn't just hear it. She felt it. It echoed through her wrist, where, one late night in Hollywood when she had strayed too far down her parents' path, a man had shattered her bone with a baseball bat, before tearing off her fishnets and stuffing them into his mouth until he gagged. She held the now motionless bird for a moment as the aching feeling faded.

The director hissed, "Throw it in the fucking pile."

Delayna nodded and did as ordered. Haste was for the best. If she spent too much time with each bird, this would take too long. She would likely be snapping crows' necks all night as it was. There were worse places she could be.

A third bird fell into her hands. She looked down to see her fingers shaking. That was unfortunate. Was she nervous? Upset? She really thought she could do this. No, she hadn't even thought about it. She had simply agreed to it, as she often did, knowing it was just a thing she needed to do to get by, and far from the worst. She hadn't killed animals before though. Not with her bare hands at least.

Still, these were crows she was exterminating. The world had enough of them. No more than insects really. Dirty, road-kill suckers, cawing belligerently and shitting all over. She shouldn't have looked at this third bird so closely though. It had a look in its eyes. Even through the sedatives it pleaded. Perhaps pleaded wasn't the right word. This was not a weak look, not a poor, pitiful begging look, but a "let me go, you fucking bitch" kind of look.

Delayna snapped its neck and threw it onto the pile.

At that first meeting with the director, he had grabbed her hands. "You have gorgeous hands. And strong forearms. Sturdy. This will do." He had asked her to get acrylic nails, silver and square-tipped, and she had done so on his dime. Not something she usually splurged on. Probably never would again.

She snapped her way through numbers four and five and six and seven quickly. She wanted to get in deep, fast. She wanted to lose count and lose herself in the process. She wanted to drift away so she would stop thinking about things like, where did the director get all these crows? She imagined the cage man, a pale young preppy, not much older than her nineteen years, running around LA with a little net. Maybe he had laid traps laced with roadkill and shiny objects—tin can lids and diamonds. Maybe the director possessed a single gleaming diamond that no crow could resist. The crows would fly toward it knowing they would be netted before they could touch it, but willing to take the risk just to get close.

She pushed the question aside, worked into a groove and finally lost count. A crow would be placed in her hands. She would wrap her right hand around the crow's head completely, covering those eyes and sealing the chomping beak. She would wrap her left hand around the bird's body, clamping the weakly flapping wings in place. Then she would twist, like opening a bottle of warm beer. Except with that snap.

She couldn't muffle that snap. It just got louder. It got so loud it seeped into her. It became one with her heartbeat and she panicked thinking that she was snapping her own heart in half. She dropped an unsnapped crow. It landed on her dirty purple sneakers, squirming and flapping impotently.

She looked up. Behind the camera, the director sweated even more than normal. His hand clenched his cock through his black dress slacks. With his other hand, he grabbed the bird and handed it back to Delayna.

"That's two-hundred and fifty," the director said through labored breaths. "Two-hundred and fifty crows out of the fucking sky."

The pile of dead birds now stood a couple feet tall and almost as wide. The director turned the camera on it for a moment, giving Delayna a brief respite. She looked around at the gray brick walls of the Burbank warehouse space and wondered what else had taken place here. What else had the director filmed?

Delayna was not in the habit of asking questions. The director had volunteered only one piece of information: "This film, it is going to make some people feel very good, and these people have a difficult time feeling good."

Delayna had merely nodded. She hadn't understood at the time, but now, seeing the placement of the director's hand and the sweat dripping from the old man's bulbous nose, she got it. It made her sad that there were men who couldn't find joy inside a woman, or even a man, and this is what it took. Not that she had ever found much joy in sex. She blamed her mother for that, for showing her that whatever mystical power intercourse held was secondary to its monetary value.

So Delayna rarely lusted for sex. When she lusted, she lusted for someone to smile at her as if sex didn't exist in the universe at all. That was hard to find. Sex seemed to sneak into every smile, with a little glimmer in the eye, a little curve of the lip. But this wasn't about her. This was about these men. She tried to frame herself as a hero, helping these poor, poor men. That gave her the momentum to snap on as the crows continued to fall into her hands.

She thought about the men and she thought about the money. Sometimes, she wondered if she should just get a real job. She didn't think she could, even if she tried. At school, she had gotten the grades that people get when they're not smart. F for failure. She had no legitimate work history. No good employer would want her. Still, she took pride in the fact that she hadn't stooped as low as her parents. As long as she didn't, she felt she was doing okay.

She snapped and she snapped until she could feel it in her wrists. Soon they started to snap too, and then there was a duet of snapping—the vibrant, hard snap of the necks over the more muted, pebbly snaps coming from where her fore-arms met her hands. She looked down and saw the black feathers stuck between her fingers, under her silver nails. She threw a dead crow onto the pile and stared at her palms. Droplets of blood seeped from where sharp beaks had pierced her skin.

The director slapped a new bird into her open hands. He said, "Five hundred. In the sky, a black cloud. On the ground here, now, a majestic mountain."

She looked at the mountain of dead birds. She thought of the food and rent money in the bank and then thought of the crows in the sky, soaring, and she wondered if the crows would smell the blood of their brethren on her hands. Would they be scared of her forever? Would they fly away to leave her without a black cloud overhead, with nothing to stop the sun from shining on her shame? She thought of her parents and how hard they'd tried to teach her to ignore thoughts like this, to fight them back and do what had to be done.

The tears trickling over her cheeks surprised her. They didn't surprise the director though. With a wave of a hand, he stopped the flow of tranquilized crows.

"Young lady," he said, his right hand still clamped on his cock. "You're almost done. You want to be done now. I can see that. But you're not going to quit, because you don't quit. You said it yourself when we first spoke. Even still, I want to remind you that you're doing something meaningful. I also want to remind you that I have an envelope in my pocket that has one thousand dollars in it, for one night of work. And you're moving fast. Faster than I thought possible. In fact, I'll offer another five hundred if you slow down for this last hundred or so. You don't have to, but the offer is there. As well as an offer of future work."

The old man gestured to continue the crow flow. A bird dropped into Delayna's hands and felt like it belonged there, a feeling akin to sniffing her own shit and finding it pleasant. She didn't like the feeling. Still, she tried to twist and snap slower, to turn the precise snaps of the birds' necks into more of a crunch, then into a grind.

The director moved from behind the camera for a moment, leaving it rolling on its tripod. He attempted to arrange the stack of dead crows into a perfect pyramid. His effort was futile. Every time he got close to perfection, a little black avalanche of dead birds left the heap lopsided.

One thousand dollars would go a long way. It would keep her from having to follow her parents' path, , at least for another month or so. One thousand dollars. One dollar per crow. One dollar per life.

Delayna snapped and twisted and twisted and snapped.

Nine-hundred and ninety-seven. Another set of eyes dimmed.

Nine-hundred and ninety-eight. Another life extinguished.
Nine-hundred and ninety-nine.

And she wondered if it was worth it. And she wondered what was more important, what she would be judged by: the weight of her sins, or the quantity.

THE SONGWRITER'S FINGERS

I REMEMBER WHEN THE SONGWRITER CAME INTO THAT LITTLE hospital, three fingers short on one hand and three extra in the palm of the other, not a tear in his eyes.

"In Japan, they can put 'em back on, good as new, I hear" he said hopefully.

"This is Waco," the doctor replied. "I can sew you up, but I can't fix you up."

I asked the songwriter if I could have his severed fingers.

He looked at me – a young nurse, the youngest working at the hospital at the time – trying to put me together like a puzzle. "What are you gonna do with 'em?"

"I'm going to put them in a jar and keep them forever."

He said I could and I did. I kept them. I kept them close.

Years later, when my brother got shot out in Dallas messing around with some bad sorts, I held that jar and thought about loss. I thought about the songwriter, dripping blood on the hospital floor and just letting his lost fingers go without a word of argument, as if he knew it would be okay. It reminded me that I would be okay, and that my brother would be okay too, in a better place without having to worry about getting money and getting other stuff he didn't need to get. Now he would get all the love imaginable, and that made all the love a sister could give seem small in comparison.

I eventually gave that love to a man named Dean, who took it and didn't even care about those green fingers I kept in the cupboard with the peanut butter and jelly jars. He just laughed and called them the old hors d'oeuvres, which he pronounced so meticulously it almost sounded wrong. We made babies and not a one of them got a grip on this world. I loved them while they were here and so did he, but when they went I let them go as easy as that, without a tear, like that songwriter and his fingers, to a better place.

It was harder when Dean got cancer. I had set myself to loving him so furiously that I breathed better every time he walked through the door of our little apartment. Ten years of that door opening and closing didn't seem nearly enough. When we walked out that door the last time to go to the hospital, I just knew he wouldn't be coming back, so I didn't close the door on my way out. I didn't want to hear the sound of it shutting, the things it said.

When I returned to that apartment alone, holding back tears for the sight of those old fingers, the place had been robbed and destroyed. I found those green fingers amidst shards of glass on the scratched linoleum and I picked them up and squeezed them so tight all the meat came off and left me clutching the bones. I asked the songwriter, "How can I just let my man go?"

I looked at those finger bones and they seemed so strong, and I knew that I didn't have a choice. Nobody had a choice in what they got to hold on to, but only in how tightly they held on to what they were given, and I had held on to my Dean so beautifully tight. I remembered that songwriter's face when I took his fingers, and how he didn't even look at them, but at his hand, and the fingers he still had.

FEED MY CORPSE TO SHARKS

It's me and Karen and Natti in my car and Natti is dead. She died last night.

Last night, the three of us were drinking wine and arm wrestling. We always arm wrestled. It weirded people out when we did it in public. They couldn't wrap their heads around it, the sight of us three girls, immaculately made up, 'cause that's how we roll, slamming each other's fists into coffee tables at house parties, bar tables. We'd try to explain it: "We're just holding hands. Very aggressively." Our nails were always fucked. It was a badge of honor. We'd get them done and then see who could get hers the gankiest the fastest. It was usually Natti.

I don't know where she got biceps like that. She hardly ever worked out. It didn't seem fair that she had muscles. She was just generally bigger than Karen and I, like 160 to our 120 each, but she carried it well on uber high heels. Boys always looked at her more than Karen or me, not that any of us paid much attention to boys when we were together. Too focused on arm wrestling and drinking wine and whatever.

But last night we stayed in, hanging out at Karen's place in downtown Boise, a shitty third floor apartment with a big window that was always wide open. That goddamn window. Between drinking and arm wrestling, Natti kept going on about fucking dudes up the ass with dildos, and trying to explain how it wasn't a power trip. She just liked seeing boys from that angle. "Because it's an empowering angle," we argued, but she wouldn't have it.

Then she somehow transitioned like this: "You know what is truly powerful? Sharks!" As she often did when she reached a certain level of drunkenness, she pulled out a crumpled brochure for a business in San Francisco that took people out shark diving. Like usual, Karen and I agreed to go with her, but only in that vague, distant future, probably never gonna happen kind of way. Natti got all dreamy eyed and said, "When I die, I want you guys to feed my corpse to sharks." We agreed that we would, but only in that vague, distant future, probably never gonna happen kind of way.

Then came the part about why Natti's dead in the back-seat of my car and we're speeding toward San Francisco blasting her shitty third-generation dubbed riot grrrl cassettes. And we're still drinking wine. Well, Natti isn't, but Karen and I sure the fuck are.

I loosen my hands on the steering wheel, realizing how hard I'm squeezing it. "I never told Natti this, but I really hate this music."

Karen takes another swig of whine straight from the bottle and giggles. "Sarah Joy, are you opening up to me?"

"It's insulting."

"It's supposed to be empowering," Karen replies.

"I know that," I snap. Then, so as not to let the sudden silence linger, I add, "I don't need girls in bands to tell me that I have self-worth, to remind me that boys are shitty and see me as a sex object. Like, duh. Why are girls telling this to girls? Shouldn't boys be telling this to boys? Where are the boy bands yelling into the faces of other boys to stop calling me a bitch and quit staring at my fucking tits?"

"Easy to say when you're thirty, but what about when you were fifteen?"

"I don't even want to talk about this," I say.

We are just outside of Reno. It's getting dark and neither of us has slept since the night before last, so we agree to find a motel. Before we get any closer to the city, I pull over to the side of I-80.

I just look toward the backseat. Natti is sitting upright, seatbelted in place, her head hanging down. With her purple hoody pulled up to cover the massive wound on the back of her head from where she collided with the concrete, she doesn't really look too dead. She looks like she's resting. With her eyes open.

Without instruction, Karen gets out and goes into the backseat. She unbuckles Natti and lays her down, covering her with blankets.

When she climbs back into the passenger seat, she's crying. I reluctantly put my hand on her shoulder. She and I have never hung out just the two of us. I've hung out with Natti without her, and she's hung out with Natti without me, but the two of us have never gone out together without Natti. Not that we're without Natti right now. But, yeah, we kind of are.

"I can't believe she's dead," I say. It seems like the sort of thing people say in these situations. I think that's what I hear when people die, even old people, even people who were not twenty-seven and in the prime of their lives. Is everyone really in such disbelief that death can happen? I don't find it all that unbelievable. First you're alive and then you're dead because something kills you, something like…

Great, now I'm crying.

Karen scrunches close to me, closing the gap between us in the front seat. She gives me a sort of sideways hug, pressing the side of her head against mine, crushing my ear against hers in a way that is totally not comforting at all.

"It wasn't your fault, Sarah Joy."

I start to wail but get choked up on the snot that has dripped down my throat during my crying jag. I kind of cough out, "I know that."

I grab a wine bottle from the floor by Karen's feet and take a sip before pulling back onto the highway to a chorus of honks from all the cars I cut off.

We stop at the first motel we find, not saying a word to each other as we check in and get situated. I plop down on one of the beds while Karen goes to the bathroom. I think about what she said about it not being my fault. Is that just another thing that people said? Would she have said that if Natti had died of lung cancer? Should I have said, "It's not your fault either," and then we could have cried in each other's arms? Or did she say that because she actually thinks it's my fault?

I don't know shit about Karen.

No, that isn't it. I know about her. I know she's got a sweet grip but weak wrists. I know she works as a bartender and is maybe a little jealous of my work-from-home web designer gig 'cause she vaguely wants to get into that. I know she likes makeup like me. She's even more obsessive about collecting weird limited edition stuff that she'll never use because she's got a look that she doesn't like to break from – a simple cat eye look. We both have kind of simple looks. I'm all about red lips. Like, bright red lips. But I still buy other shades. I also know she likes breaking up with boys almost as much as she likes making out with boys, like me.

We've learned that we have these things in common, more through Natti than through direct conversation, but I don't know what drives them in her. It's like we speak two different languages, and Natti was always the translator, helping us understand each other. Without Natti, I have no fucking clue how this bitch's brain works. Is she even going to the bathroom right now? For all I know, she could be in there phoning space aliens to beam her up to whatever "it's not your fault" planet she came from.

She comes out of the bathroom and says, "I bet we're not the first people to stay at this motel with a corpse."

Part of me wants to tell her that it's stupid to even think about other people and their corpses when we don't know what the fuck we're doing with our own corpse drama, but for the sake of diplomacy, I feign a giggle and agree.

"This place does have a 'corpses welcome' sort of vibe, doesn't it?" I say.

"Maybe it's better this way," Karen says.

I don't get the statement. I look at my nails. Hardly chipped at all. "What?" I ask, trying not to sound like I'm arguing, even though I'm really arguing.

"What if the soul isn't this ethereal thing that immediately detaches from the body upon death. What if it's actually linked to the flesh?"

"I don't know if I believe in souls."

Karen takes a swig of wine and passes the bottle to me. "You're thinking of the soul as some sort of quasi-supernatural entity, like a ball of light that floats out of you when you die. Maybe it's more physical, and it can't leave the body until the flesh fully decays and goes back into the earth. All the bodies trapped underground in fancy decay-proof coffins are still clinging to their souls."

"That seems logical, but also sad." I don't want to think about my grandparents' souls sitting six feet under, unable to get to heaven or wherever souls go, so I say, "We're just meat."

"Fuck you," Karen says.

We sit in silence. I stare at the print hanging above the bed. It depicts a dirt path winding through a garden filled with pastel flowers. A romantic notion flits through me and I imagine that those flowers are what souls look like, pink and round, but then I decide that's kind of gross.

"So by feeding Natti to sharks, we're setting her soul free?" I ask.

"That's what I'm saying," Karen says, still hardened.

"Okay."

I climb under the blankets fully clothed in the T-shirt and pink pajama pants I've been wearing since I got to Karen's last night. I pretend to fall asleep but don't sleep at all.

I'm out of bed at sunrise the next morning. Karen is actually legitimately sleeping, so I step out of the room, cross the parking lot and go into the motel office to grab a plate full of the stale bagels and bruised apples they refer to as a "continental breakfast."

When I return to the room, Karen rolls out of bed and says, "If Natti's not going to shower, I'm not going to shower."

"I won't either then. We will see who stinks the most."

Back in the car, we discover that Natti has won this contest too. I don't say anything, but I'm pretty sure some shit came out of her overnight. This smell is not going to leave my car for a long time, maybe ever. Maybe it will be Natti's way of haunting me.

Karen reminisces as we drive. She talks about arm wrestling. She muses about various boys that stumbled away after bringing drinks to our table, only to have us push the drinks out of the way so we could slam each other's fists against the tabletop, cracking nails. "Why is that so intimidating?"

I think about that for a second. "It's less that it was intimidating and more that we were completely ignoring the boys."

"You don't think men are intimidated by strong women?" she asks.

"Are we strong women?" I reply.

"How did you meet Natti?" Karen asks.

"This is a good story! I was at a bar with this boy from work. First date. We were standing next to each other in silence. Our conversation had devolved into me asking him if he liked this or that, and vice versa. I would ask, 'Do you like football?' and he'd say, 'No.' Then he'd ask, 'Do you like horror movies?' and I'd say, 'No.' We just went through a checklist and found that we literally had nothing in common.

"We ended up kind of blocking the entrance to the restrooms. Most people were saying excuse me or squeezing between us, but then this monster blonde with tattooed arms and fifty-inch high heels stomped up to us. She looked at this dude and she looked at me. She smiled at me as if she had just totally read what was going on, and then she asked the dude, 'Do you like to suck cock?'"

"Oh yeah, I've heard this story before," Karen interrupts.

"Yeah," I say, kind of wishing I could finish the story anyway.

I wonder if I should ask Karen how she met Natti, just so she can say it out loud, even though I know they met while working at the same restaurant, Natti waitressing and Karen bartending. Something about beef tacos.

Before I get the chance, Karen says, "We probably should stop for gas?"

I look at the gas gauge, near empty, and nod.

I pull into the next gas station. There's a kid, a teenage boy, hugging one of the pumps. I curse under my breath, so caught up in conversation I forgot that these gas station stops can't be normal gas station stops. I go to a different pump to avoid the boy, but he skips over to my car. Before I can get out to try to shoo him away, he's already jammed the nozzle into my gas tank.

He jumps in front of my door to prevent me from getting out. "Full service, ma'am!"

Confused, I stare at him. He stares back at me, as if I'm supposed to understand what he's saying. I don't and I hate the way he's looking at me. Still, I need him to keep staring at me, not to look into the backseat. I need him to keep his eyes locked on mine, so I keep mine locked on his.

He gets the wrong idea, winks and repeats, "Full service here, ma'am."

I turn away and whisper to Karen, "What does that mean?"

"You've never been to a full-service station, Sarah Joy?" Karen asks.

"I guess not."

She shrugs. "They put the gas in for you. You can ask him to check your oil and wash your windshield too, if you want."

"No," I try not to raise my voice. "I definitely do not want, Karen."

"Oh. Yeah."

I look at the kid. He's not wearing any sort of uniform. Torn jeans. Worn out tie-dyed T-shirt. "Do you think he even works here?"

The kid presses his face against the backseat window. Then he's in my window, gesturing for me to roll it down. I do, about halfway. He squeezes his face into the opening.

"Oh god, I think he's feral," Karen whispers, looking away.

"Is she okay?" the kid asks. "In the backseat there?"

"Yes," I reply. "Just under the weather."

I see his nostrils working as he sniffs, a bunch of little sniffs, then a big one. He moves back and I start to roll the window up, but before I do he shoves his face into the opening again. Louder now, insistent, the kid says, "You need to check her. She don't smell right. That's not an under-the-weather smell."

"I promise she's fine, but we do need to get going."

I roll up the window a bit more. The kid jams his fingers

in, clutches the glass, pulls down with all his weight. "That's a dead body!" the he shouts, pointing into the backseat. "You're transporting a dead body across state lines!"

I almost laugh at the way he makes it sound like an official thing.

Karen replies, "Be quiet! She's just sleeping!"

The kid looks through the back window again. He shakes his head so hard I can almost feel it. "Nah. She's dead."

I twist around to see what the kid sees. Natti's face is peeking out between her purple hoody and the blanket. Her eyes are open and dry looking. Her mouth is open too, and her tongue is floating in there, like it's getting ready to levitate out. Maybe that's where the soul is. I can't argue with the kid. Natti definitely looks dead.

"Can I touch her?" the kid asks.

Before I can answer, the gas pump clicks off and the kid moves away. For a moment, I think the interaction is over, but then he slides his hand in my window, palms up, fingers wiggling. "It will be thirty-one dollars and twelve cents plus tip," he says. Then he smiles, "Or it's free if you let me touch that body."

"No way," I say.

"Just let the freak do it." Karen reaches back to unlock the door.

"Fine, but make it quick," I say.

I assume the kid is just going to open the door and give poor Natti a quick poke and that will be that. Then I look in the rearview mirror and see that he has crawled all the way in and is lying on top of her. His face is inches from hers. He grabs her thick lower lip between the thumbs and pointer fingers of each hand and pulls it down to get a good look at her lower teeth.

"I thought the gums were supposed to turn black and oozy?" he asks.

"Get the fuck out of the car now!" I shout.

Karen is cracking up.

The kid doesn't move, just keeps poking around in Natti's mouth.

I turn and swat the kid. I end up slapping his ass. He looks at me and smiles. As he pushes himself off Natti, he squeezes her boobs. I can't tell if it's intentional or not, but I keep swatting him until he's out of the car. Then I hit the gas.

In the rearview mirror, I watch as the kid bolts away from the gas pumps, chased by someone working inside the station.

"That kid didn't even work there," I say.

Karen laughs. I don't actually think it's that funny. We are, in fact, transporting a dead body across state lines. We could probably go to jail.

"Even when she's dead, Natti gets all the fucking attention!" Karen says.

Now I laugh. It's true. Natti would have loved that.

I put in another one of Natti's riot grrrl tapes. Maybe I need to stop thinking about things so hard and just have fun. If a girl can't have fun while driving to California with her dead best friend while listening to nineties music, then a girl just can't have fun at all. I vomit a little in my mouth and the regurgitated wine tastes as cheap coming up as it did going down.

I try to talk to Karen, but I've run out of things to say. I catch myself starting to ask her if there's any specific food she'd like to eat while we're in San Francisco, but I stop myself because I can't imagine any answer that wouldn't be super inane. I decide that uncomfortable silence beats forced conversation.

I let some screaming lady fill the void. She's got a valley girl accent. I know most of these songs by heart. In my head, I hear Natti singing along. She was a terrible singer. Whenever she sang, I felt like the joints in my body had been forced to bend the wrong way. I felt like someone had sprayed lemon juice on my tongue, and I think the face I made probably reflected that, which was why Natti always sang louder.

I start to sing under my breath. When the song comes to the chorus, I sing a little louder. I can feel Karen staring at me.

"You don't even like this music," she says.

I keep singing.

On the next song, Karen sings too. Her voice is high, and she tries too hard to nail every one of the singer's affectations. Our voices don't mesh, sandpaper layered over scouring pads. I forget the lyrics and just kind of hit the notes. Then I fall back and hum a little before shutting my mouth.

Karen's pointer fingers become drumsticks and she pounds out a beat on the dashboard, except it's not really the beat that's happening in the song.

"How much longer do you think?" she asks.

I inadvertently press the gas pedal down. "An hour or so."

"This is probably illegal," Karen says.

"What is?"

"All of this."

WHEN WE GET to the docks, Karen covers Natti up so her body isn't spotted while we go look for the shark boat, the one from the brochure, the one Natti picked out. As we walk along, I ask Karen if we should come up with a plan.

"For what?"

"For convincing the boat guy to do this?"

"I don't think that's something we can plan," she replies, walking faster.

I don't really see how it's something we can not plan, but I don't actually have a plan in mind, so I just follow her.

We find a sign that says "Swim With Sharks!" It has an

arrow pointed toward a boat. The arrow is painted like a candy cane. I wonder if this is a Christmas tradition in San Francisco, swimming with sharks. Do people dress up as elves and dive in with handfuls of chum? I picture the elves being eaten alive and remember that it's not so much swimming as it is being lowered into the water in a cage. At least, that's how the brochure described it.

We make our way to a walkway that leads onto the boat. The walkway is also painted with candy cane trimmings.

"Hello!" Karen yells.

A middle-aged man crawls out from the bowels of the boat. He's got a big head that he's obviously shaved bare because he is mostly balding.

"You girls got reservations?" he asks.

"No," I say.

"The boat only runs at certain times," he says, as if the boat itself is the mastermind behind the schedule and it wouldn't possibly agree to a deviation.

"We can pay." As I say this, I realize we probably can't actually pay that much at all. I don't even know what the regular price is.

"Girlie, the boat only goes out with a dozen or more shark swimmers."

The man starts to climb back into his boat hole.

"We can do things for you," Karen says.

I freeze.

So does the man. "What kind of... things?"

My question exactly.

Karen looks at me, as if it's my turn to explain. I know what things she's talking about. She's talking about the things Natti would do if she were in this situation, except Natti would never actually do those things. Natti talked like a perv, but she was a lot more innocent than she pretended to be. Sure, she drilled some dudes in the b-holes with dildos, but that usually happened when she was deep in a relationship.

She didn't just offer sex to sailors at random. Was this guy a sailor?

I say, "Like chores and stuff."

Karen elbows me hard. "And other things!" she shouts.

"Why don't you just book a reservation online and come back tomorrow morning," the man says. "Save yourself from these 'things' you speak of."

This man is not the type of man who will trade sex for shark swimming excursions, so it dawns on me that he is probably not the type of man who will dump a dead body in the ocean. I wonder if there are other boats. I don't want to have sex with a sailor. I don't want Karen to have sex with a sailor. But I think we need to find a sailor who wants to have sex with us if we are going to get anywhere, so I start to walk away.

Karen grabs me by the arm and pulls me back.

I shake free of her grip. "What? He won't help us."

"Yes, he will."

"Will I now?" The man is almost fully in his boat hole, only his head visible.

"Dude," she says to the man, "this is very complicated, so can you just listen?"

The man grunts, crawls fully out of his boat hole and leans against the edge of the boat, arms crossed, his invitation for Karen to continue.

"We have this friend," Karen says.

"Natalia," I say her name. "Natti."

"Did you know that your soul is basically glued to your flesh? It is stuck there. It may be invisible, but it's in there with your blood and your tendons. If you put all of it in a box underground and seal it up tight, it isn't going anywhere."

The man looks puzzled, so I interrupt and add, "Our friend needs to go. Her soul needs to go where it's supposed to go."

"Your friend?" the man asks.

"Natti. She doesn't want to be buried. She wants to be fed to sharks," I say.

He waves his hand at us as if swatting away a fly, as if swatting away a wad of bullshit that has been thrown at his face. His scowl makes it seem as though the wad of shit actually hit him and he is forcing himself to chew on it.

Karen jumps into the boat and gets between the man and his boat hole. I stomp up the plank after her and grab the man by his arm. I try to think of something that Natti would say. Natti would charm this man. She would charm this man with perversion, and he would blush, and she would throw him off the boat with her big, strong, tattooed arms and drive out into the ocean without him.

I consider throwing the man off the boat because I can't think of any words that Natti would say, and that makes me sad, like how could I not have memorized them? But the man is a foot taller than me and weighs as much as Karen and I combined, so sending him overboard is probably not an option.

"She's already dead," I repeat. "She just wants to be fed to sharks."

He looks at me now like he's going to throw me overboard. I squeeze tightly on to his arm. If I'm going in, I'm taking him with me. Karen grabs his other arm and starts to push toward the side of the boat. She actually wants to push him in. What is she thinking? We don't even know how to drive a boat! This is crazy!

I push against her at first, and then I pull. The man resists, planting his feet hard on the deck of the boat. I pull harder. I will do this for Natti.

The man shakes free with little effort and laughs.

"Where is your friend?" he asks.

"In the car," Karen says. She's crying. I'm crying.

The man shakes his head, accenting the fact that he is

going against his better judgment. "In the grand scheme, I guess it don't make any difference if she's put to rest in the dirt or at sea. Given the choice, I'd prefer at sea myself. Maybe not in the mouths of sharks, but… Let's go get her."

Karen leads the man back to my car. I notice how many people are coming and going. I get paranoid that someone is going to see us moving Natti's body. But the man doesn't seem worried, so I don't say anything.

I open the back door of the car and the man says, "She's a whopper," but not in a negative way, more like in a way that someone says when they catch a big fish. I don't even think he's talking about her physically. I think he's talking about her personality. Natti is a whopper. Was a whopper. But he didn't know her, so I kind of mutter, "Fuck off," under my breath, but he doesn't hear me.

The man grabs Natti under her arms. Karen and I each carry one of Natti's feet. She smells bad. Even with the blanket covering her, she's unmistakably a human body. People walk by without even looking twice. Do they honestly think we're bringing supplies or something to the boat? Do people just not see things?

We walk down the dock and across the plank to the boat, placing Natti's blanket-covered body on the deck. The man scurries away, dragging the plank into the boat and untying the ropes that anchor the boat to the dock.

I pull the blanket down so Natti can see the sky above.

The man turns the boat on and we push out into the ocean.

"I think I smell the sharks already," Karen says.

"That's sea lion shit," the man shouts from his post at the steering wheel.

I whisper, "I don't think it is. I think it's sharks."

"How far out do we need to go?" Karen asks.

"Pretty far, all things considered," the man says.

Karen and I both nod.

The two of us move to opposite sides of the deck and stare at the waves. I've never seen the ocean before. It's pretty vast. I'm supposed to think it's pretty vast. I'm supposed to get chills looking at the water going on and on. Really though, I don't think I care right now. Natti would be bummed.

No, Natti wouldn't give a shit. She'd say something that shrank it all down and everyone would laugh. Then she'd blow it back up again and everyone would smile. Then she'd say something about cocks.

Fuck.

San Francisco gets farther away. The sun dips its fiery toes into the water.

"Will we be there soon?" I ask.

The man grunts in a way that I take to mean yes.

I look at Natti's body. Her blonde hair is all messed up. Her eyes are wide. She looks like she just got super high and had sex. Except for the blood.

"It was so weird," Karen says. She's crying.

We're in the middle of the ocean. Not really though. But we're far enough.

"Natti's mom is going to kill us when she finds out about this, Sarah Joy."

I wonder if we're doing the right thing. Then I look at Natti's face, and I imagine it in a coffin, just trapped, trying to get out to wherever the fuck her soul is going to go. I can't stand it.

"She's going to blame us for everything," I say.

Karen nods.

"Are we to blame?" I ask.

Karen looks at me. She quickly looks away and says, "Not... we."

"Wait, do you think I'm to blame?"

"You're the one that chased her."

I scream, "I didn't chase her!"

"She was drunk. We were all drunk. It was an accident," Karen says.

"It was an accident," I say.

The boat motor stops and there's too much silence. The man fills it by stomping his feet around the deck, finally standing over Natti.

"Now would be a good time for the eulogy," he says.

"The eulogy," I echo, turning to Karen. "Do we have a eulogy?"

Karen shrugs.

The man looks down at Natti. "She's young."

"Twenty-seven," I say.

"Young," he repeats. "Did she have children?"

Karen and I both laugh.

"Oh my god," Karen shrieks through her laughter. "I can picture it. Natti chasing a bunch of rugrats as they run through the house."

I do my best Natti impression: "Stay out of my dildo drawer, you brats!"

The man looks at us like we're on something. I wish we were. I wish we hadn't left the wine in the car. Isn't that a part of boating? Don't we have to smash a wine bottle on the deck or something?

The man has something better than wine: a big bucket full of bloody meat. For a second, he looks like he's going to hand it to me or Karen. Then he thinks better of it and hurls it into the water himself. It plops into the ocean and spreads out like a wine stain on a white blouse, except redder. A lot redder.

"What kind of sharks are here? Hammerheads?" I ask.

"Nah. No hammerheads," he says. "These waters here, you've got your calypso sharks, your zydeco sharks, your rasta-tone sharks. These waters here, you've got the sharks that really like to dance."

"Natti would have known all about those sharks," I say.

"No, she wouldn't have," Karen says, pointing a scowl at the man. "Those aren't real sharks. He's fucking with us."

Shark heads break out of the water, gobbling up chum as if it was trying to flee. Great whites with impenetrably black eyes. They look mad. There are a lot of teeth. I count nine sharks. Probably nine hundred teeth.

"Why do people want to swim with sharks?" I ask.

"Ask your friend here." The man pokes Natti with the tip of his boot.

"We should throw her in now," Karen says.

"I don't like that," I say. "I don't like 'throw her in.'"

"What should we say instead?" Karen asks.

"Let's just let her swim."

The man crouches down to pick Natti up, but Karen and I shoo him away. We don't need his help now. Each of us grabs her under one of her arms and we drag her to the side of the boat. We kind of pull her up so she's sitting with her back against the side. Then we count to three and hoist her over.

I panic and try to hold her back, not ready to let her go, but her weight and the momentum are too great. She tumbles over the side of the boat and splashes down into the bloody water. She sinks underneath for a second and then bobs up to the surface. Her eyes stay open the whole time. A thin layer of ocean water pools over them. Her mouth is still wide open. She is sticking her tongue out at us.

The sharks circle around her. They nose through the bloody water. They snatch up the last bits of chum. Natti's body floats amidst them, bobbing up and down on the waves. The setting sun reflects off the water in one bright, straight line – a path away from the boat. The waves carry Natti along that path.

The sharks stay with her, but they don't touch her. She just floats with them. Their fins cut through the water around her, circling her, protecting her.

Natti moves farther and farther away with the waves.

Her arms spread wide, ready to hold everything, ready to hold all of it.

ROLLED UP

I'M ROLLED UP INSIDE A DIRTY SHAG RUG IN THE GRAFFITI-covered alley behind the club. A band is loading in, and they have to step on me to get from their van to the back door. Their footsteps carry the extra weight of their gear. It feels so good.

They don't know I'm here. That would ruin it. When people know I'm underfoot, their steps become too intentional. They avoid me, tiptoe lightly over me or stomp extra hard. It doesn't feel natural. It's better when they don't know.

A few people know I'm here of course. Rolling myself up in a rug and dragging myself to the backstage entrance of a seedy East Village punk club is not an option, so I have an arrangement with a couple guys to get me here and then unroll me at the end of the night. Plus there are a few regulars who got curious about the rolled up rug that appears in different places around the club a few times a week, so stained from footprints and grime that the orange and brown pattern is barely discernable. Not to mention the one woman whose high heel hit that sweet spot on my neck, right under my jaw, eliciting a groan of pleasure I couldn't contain. She unrolled me and kicked the shit out of me with those heels, calling me a pervert.

I'm not a pervert though. This isn't a fetish for me. It's not that simple. I don't get off on it sexually. How could I? Jacking off isn't an option when I'm rolled up so tight my arms are pinned to my sides. I get off on it emotionally. Sometimes it's so intense I cry, not because of the pain, but because of how it makes me feel. It's not like an out of body thing, not exactly, because I'm very much present in my self. However, my senses reach beyond the boundaries of my flesh. I may not be able to see, but I can feel and hear and smell everything that is happening around me, even if it's muffled. I'm omniscient in my rug.

Oh, there is the physical sensation too. It isn't painful, although I'm often left bruised and I have a permanent limp from an untreated ankle fracture. It's not like getting kicked. The rug dulls the impact, so it's just the weight, the pressure. I love the feel of feet hitting different parts of me. The weight of a body on my buttocks or where the back of my skull meets my spine sends heat through my veins.

That heat dissipates quickly after the band members grunt through the last of their load-in. I'm left only with the external heat. It's a warm night, and the rug amplifies the warmth. I'm sweating. My naked flesh is chafing against the rug backing. When I unroll, my skin will be red and imprinted with the blocky pattern. But I can't think about unrolling now. The evening has just begun.

The backstage door is closed with a click and suddenly there is silence. New York City silence, at least. This is the city that never sleeps, after all. It's alive at all hours. Or is it? The whir of traffic, shoes scuttling over sidewalks, conversations, music in the distance. The same people going the same places and doing the same things. I hear it every night, and it sounds so mechanical, so routine. Is this city as wild and alive as it promises, or are the routines just a little more exciting?

When the band starts to play, the back door cannot contain the music. It's that newer, faster version of punk. I've been coming here for eight years, more or less. Time isn't something I pay attention to. But I've been coming since the late '70s, and I'm amazed at how much this music has evolved in such a short time. I can't say I love it. I grew up in Tennessee listening to country before I hitchhiked here in the '60s. But I love the people. They are artsy and curious.

This new strain of punk though, this hardcore, it's especially exciting. Once in a while I'll actually come to the club to see a band, if I can scrounge up the bills. When these hardcore bands play, the crowds do a thing they call slam dancing. They stomp and spin and smash into each other. I can't help but wish I could lay my rug right there in front of the stage and be part of it in my own way. Maybe someday.

The set is over fast and the band comes out once again to step on me. They are practically bouncing they are so energized. Their sweaty shirtless chests slap against each other as they give hard hugs. "Did you see how crazy that crowd was? They were jumping off the stage! I could have played all night!" Their BO is so strong it wafts down to me and I draw it in through my nostrils. They keep stepping on me because they cannot stand still. They don't know what to do with themselves.

The gruff voice of the club owner echoes out. "Clear the stage, assholes!"

They laugh and get to work, and once again I absorb those extra weighted steps. The heat in me is so intense it reaches out of my skin, penetrating the rug. Purple flames light up the darkness behind my eyelids.

My euphoria is cancelled out by a scent that swirls past my nose. Something smells off. It's not my BO, nor that of the band members. It's not the standard stink of the East Village, with its piles of garbage and unclean bodies packed together. Something truly smells off, like meat gone wet with rot.

The footsteps stop.

Wait, I hear one set of footsteps approaching. They come in an odd, stumbling cadence. Drunken footsteps, I think.

"Hey lady, are you okay?" one of the band members asks.

"What's wrong with her fucking face?" another whispers.

"It looks like it's falling off."

"Do you need an ambulance?"

There's a long pause and then an answer: "Amaraaaaaghhh!"

This last cry puts pins in my spine. There's so much pain in it, and anger, and... need? Hunger? I've never heard anything like it. The shuffling, off-kilter steps grow closer and the members of the band back up until they are all standing on me —one on my head, one on my upper back, one on my butt and one on my calves. I am their ground. I can feel them shaking. Their fear shakes down into me.

Another cry from the encroaching woman, and suddenly weight shifts above me. She has knocked one of the band members down and they are struggling on the rug. Their bodies move back and forth over me like a rolling pin.

"Get her off," her victim pleads.

The snapping of teeth is so loud, even louder than the thuds of a blunt object – a microphone stand maybe – against flesh. This has never happened before. I have never been beneath a bar fight. But is this a bar fight? Shouting, heavy breathing, blows to bodies, yes – but that gnashing of teeth? Who fights like that?

Now the teeth are not just clicking against each other. They have found something to latch onto. Human meat. I know that blood is soaking into my rug. This woman, is she a cannibal? Has she killed a member of the band? I listen for the others. I listen hard over the sound of chewing, but hear nothing. Did they flee into the club like cowards while their friend was eaten alive?

The pressure on my rug eases and I try to get control of

my thoughts, because they don't make sense. Perhaps I dozed off and had a strange little nightmare. In the hot, dark cocoon of my rug, sometimes awake and asleep blend together. But no; I can still feel the rug against my skin, the warm air through my nostrils as I inhale. I'm awake.

I laugh loudly. Too loudly. Maybe I want to be heard right now. Maybe I need to be unrolled and brought back into reality. And my laugh does get a response: scraping at my rug, the frantic scratching of fingernails against shag. Another sickening cry from this woman and I am suddenly scared.

I take a deep breath and my eyes water at the scent I pull in. It is the scent of death. I know that scent well. I live in a squat, not far from the club. A tower of tagged and broken bricks filled with drunks and junkies who die regularly and are rarely discovered in a timely manner. I once found an overdose case with needle in arm who had decayed so badly I wasn't sure if it was a man or a woman. I wrapped my hands in plastic bags and pulled that body down four flights of steps and across three city blocks to a dumpster where it could be found without bringing police into my home. All the way I sucked in the odor.

The smell now is even stronger, too strong to be coming from the dead band member above me or from the woman who attacked him. It's getting closer, carried by feet, many feet that drag loose against blacktop. Bare toes catch on potholes and cracks. Ankles twist and snap. I hear bodies fall and the farcical movement that might have been called walking gives way to crawling. I do not have to see to know that these are dead people, and they are coming.

Within seconds they are on me, and as hard as I try to convince myself that I am wrong, I cannot deny my senses. The death stink grips my stomach hard and bile bubbles up my throat. I choke it down as the dead gather above.

So many feet on my rug. They must be packed body to body, pressing against each other as they push against the back door of the club. I hear groans and decaying flesh banging against metal, scraping against brick. With each scratch, fingernails flip free and the last bits of flesh on fingertips peel away.

My spine cracks. Something pops in my shoulder. I have never had so much weight on me at once. I have to fight to breathe, but I cannot deny how good this feels. I'm being pressed into nothingness, but I am still here. And what would happen if I weren't? I'm the glue that bonds these maggoty feet to the Earth. Without me, they would float up into the night sky and explode.

I swear I can feel a crack make its way through my right forearm bone and I envision blue flames in the fissure. Those flames run through me, up to my skull, where there is another rupture on my left temple. Turn me to dust! Let me blow through this alleyway to live under the foot of every New Yorker!

A squeal of metal tells me the backstage door is being forced open against the weight of the walking dead mob.

"There's at least a hundred of them," a voice says.

"Can we push through?" another asks.

"We don't have a choice. Take this."

"A yardstick?"

"Well, I'm using the bat. I'll go first."

Wood strikes decaying flesh and the weight shifts above me. With every blow, the odor of death gets more powerful. Skulls are opened to release the gasses that have accumulated around fetid brains. It's so strong it sticks to the inside of my mouth and I can practically chew on it like gum. It blends with the taste of blood. Where am I bleeding from? Inside? Or did my teeth merely rip my cheeks?

The wild swinging causes the crowd of corpses to part, putting more weight on my head and my legs. Quick steps volley off my midsection as a small group of living people make their way through. I consider crying for help, but it would be useless. If my cry was even able to penetrate my rug and the anxious clacking of corpse teeth, what could those few living do? Drag me away from here? Away from the ecstasy of all these feet above me? As much as I know that my body is crumbling – Ah, there goes my other hip – I cannot concede. Let it crumble in ecstasy. There is no life after this.

The scent of death becomes overwhelming. This is a scent without a home. The bodies are decaying and can no longer hold it, so it swirls desperately through the air to me so I can suck it into my lungs and give it a new place to live.

There's a sound like meat being slapped into the display case at the deli, and then like a bucket of not-quite-liquid hitting blacktop. Insides are pouring out, and now there's a wetness to the clacking of dead teeth, a new slurping. And that moaning, there's an all-too-familiar tone there. Could they be experiencing the level of joy that I'm experiencing right now? There's a whipping against my rug, and I imagine intestines at the center of a tug of war, yellowed nails piercing the tissue and setting free the brown muck inside. The dead are no longer standing on me. They are writhing around above me, against each other. Movement is constant.

Did any of the living survive? I think not. If they had, the dead would have given chase. I hear a cracking from my torso. A rib, most likely. There's a stabbing when I breathe. Perhaps several ribs are broken. That's fine. How high are the dead piled above me? Three bodies deep at least. Five? Twenty? Am I at the bottom of a skyscraper of squirming dead New Yorkers? The thought almost takes me out of my body, to the top of this skyscraper. I live in every dead body brick that makes it. I am the foundation, and without me it is nothing. Tower into space on me.

The dead are roaring above me, and the air is growing thin. They have blocked off all oxygen. I am so wet. This is not just my sweat. My bones have burst through my body. I am truly being crushed! Outside viscera has soaked through the rug and now coats me too. I can feel its warm redness, lubing my body under this impossible weight. Has any human ever felt a sensation like this before?

My pierced lungs suck in a big breath. I can breathe again. No! My load is getting lighter. My tower is collapsing. Knees scraped to bone slide against blacktop away from me, a new excitement in their groaning. Something is calling them away. They are leaving, all of them, after some new ecstasy, taking mine away.

A skittering above me indicates one lingering corpse fingering through the matted shag of my rug in hopes of finding a bit of liver or brain, but even that one is soon gone and there is nothing above me aside from that hollow weight of my rug, my sacred shell. I've never felt such loss. Everything so quickly turned to nothing.

Nothing. A naked, broken man wrapped up in a rug in an alley.

I know that my unrollers are gone. Eaten alive or fled. I'm not getting out of here. I don't want to get out of here. There is no life for me after this.

It's done. At least it's done here. In the distance though: Alarms. Sirens. Doors slamming. Gunshots. Screams. This is New York City, and I swear to Christ it has never sounded more alive.

HUNTRESS

GARI PULLED THE BOWSTRING TAUT AND AIMED AT THE BUCK barreling toward her. She hadn't expected it to happen like this. She'd expected to stumble onto a docile animal, grazing, waiting patiently for her arrow. But something in the woods had spooked the deer and now it leapt in Gari's direction, not seeing her crouched behind a boulder. She felt the tension of her weapon through her fingers, her forearm, her shoulder, her back. This was why she loved the bow. It was so intricately tied to how she moved, how she breathed – an extension of her body.

She breathed deep and took in the majesty of the buck. He was beautiful, over 300 pounds, with a rack so big it knocked branches from trees as he ran. She kept her sight on his chest, knowing she couldn't release the arrow with the deer coming at her like this. Too much muscle and bone to get through. Too little chance of a kill. She needed him to turn so she could hit him broadside, a lethal shot. But he didn't. He kept coming, until he bounded past the boulder she hid behind and away.

She relaxed her body and the bow.

A rustling ahead drew her attention. Before she could

draw the bowstring back again she caught sight of the blaze orange jacket. Her brother's jacket.

"You spooked him." She stood, stretched her legs.

"I drove him right to you!"

She saw no point in arguing with Chuck. He'd been deer hunting since he was ten, joining their dad and grandfather every season. To Chuck, Gari's archery record was meaningless in the woods.

This was her first season. Nobody had invited her, but after 30 years of watching the men in her family go off into the woods on what they always made out to be a mystic adventure, she invited herself. Chuck had tried to talk her out of it, telling her it's a guy thing, drinking and dirty jokes, and he wasn't going to be able to protect her, which was funny because he'd never protected her. She didn't take no for an answer. It was 1987 and a woman could hunt if she wanted to.

"Sun's setting," Chuck said. "Let's go back to the cabin and see if the boys are there yet."

They crunched through fallen leaves, weaved around raspberry brambles. Gari wasn't looking forward to meeting the boys. She'd overheard her brother's phone conversations with them and knew they were not pleased. He'd resorted to telling them she was gay and thus one of the guys. She hadn't loved being outed that way, but it had worked and she now had her first day of hunting under her belt.

The log cabin sat tucked away on a driveway that was more grass than gravel. Her father had helped her grandfather build it when he was a kid, back in the 1940s, on this hundred acre parcel of perfect Driftless Wisconsin hunting land that had been in the family five generations. The cabin was nothing fancy. She could fit two of them in her Minneapolis apartment. But it was sturdy, with thick oak logs that could withstand a tank attack. Smoke billowed from the stone chimney, so the boys had been there long enough to start a fire.

Inside, the flames cast an orange hue on the four mounted deer heads that adorned the walls, the largest catch from each generation. In the center, a massive taxidermied black bear head, caught in a roar, the date her grandfather killed it scrawled in blood red on the wooden base. She'd never been here, never set foot in these woods until now, but she'd seen pictures and heard stories, knew about each of these trophies. Before the weekend was over, she would add a head to that wall.

Three men sat on an old couch. Her brother introduced them as Todd, Daniel and Big Chuck. "I'm known as Little Chuck out here," he clarified, "to avoid confusion."

She'd never thought of her brother at little, nearly six feet to her five and a half, but Big Chuck was something else. Even sitting on the couch, she could tell he was at least six and a half feet.

"I'm Gari," she introduced herself to the staring men.

"Oh yeah, this is my sister," Chuck added, as if her name wasn't important.

"Never met a gal with that name before," Big Chuck said.

"It's short for Garibella," she replied, taking off her blaze orange jacket, a hand-me-down from her father, "but that name got too delicate for me."

Big Chuck nodded. "Yeah, I can see that."

She sat cross-legged on the floor close to the fire as her brother cracked open a beer. She unzipped her bow case to slide her bow in.

"Let me see your bow, Gari." Todd reached out, making give-me gestures with his fingers. "I've never looked at a lady's bow before."

"It's not a lady's bow." Gari ignored the man's grabbing fingers, determined not to let him fiddle with her weapon. "My grandpa used this bow on his last few hunting trips. It's a regular compound bow. Well, one of the first compound bows really."

She'd been secretly using that bow since she was eight. Whenever she stayed with her grandpa, she'd wait for him to get absorbed in his reading. Then she'd sneak into the garage, take out the bow and try to pull the string back. She couldn't at first, and that had prompted her to start doing pullups and pushups. By the time she was ten, she could pull the string back easily, but it still took another couple years before she worked up the guts to nock an arrow.

When her grandpa passed away a few years later, nobody noticed his bow go missing. She'd hidden it in her closet behind boxes of old schoolwork. She'd been so convinced that it was for men, and that somehow she was wrong in wanting to use it. She didn't want people to see her doing anything masculine, because then they might realize she was gay, which she wasn't even able to put into words at the time. Eventually Gari realized she didn't have to hide her love of archery, even joined a club at school. It took her a little longer to realize she didn't have to hide her love of women.

Todd stood from the couch. "Let's go to Jack's."

"Yeah!" Daniel shouted. "Let's get some pussy!"

Todd laughed. "Daniel, you aren't any better at getting pussy than you are at getting deer."

"Shouldn't talk like that with a lady around," Big Chuck said.

Todd replied, "What I hear, she likes to get pussy too."

Gari didn't say anything. As much as their talk made her cringe, she let them have it. She had no interest in being treated like one of the guys, but it was better than being treated like an outsider. She glanced at her brother. He shrugged, gave her a told-you-so look.

She didn't want to go to the bar. She'd only known the boys a few minutes and already craved alone time. Nothing would make her happier than sitting in the loft bunk, lighting a couple candles and reading one of the mangled Hustlers stacked in the corner. But the weekend would go better if she played along, and part of her was curious what these guys did out here when it was too dark to hunt.

They drove to a bar and grill with a Labrador on the sign. Was the Labrador Jack or did Jack's pet? Trucks packed the parking lot, a couple with dead deer in the beds. She looked at one as she followed the boys into the bar. A small rack buck, tongue lolled out. She would kill something bigger. No victory in picking off a baby.

Cigarette smoke poured from the bar when they opened the door. Gari stepped inside after the boys and paused for her eyes to adjust to the burning. The bar was bustling, mostly with men as Gari expected. Near the jukebox though, she noticed a woman in dirty coveralls with work gloves hanging from the back pocket. Not the typical night-on-the-town outfit. The woman watched Gari walk in with the boys and Gari wondered if she might have a good night after all.

She got a shot of whiskey to embolden her. The woman in the grimy overalls made her jukebox pick – a country song, not a loving one like Gari had expected, but a fighting one – and sauntered back to the bar. The empty stools on either side of her boded well.

Gari leaned in next to the woman, waited for eye contact.

"You looking at me?" the woman asked.

"I can't tell if you're a lesbian or just from Wisconsin."

Violence flashed across the woman's eyes and for a moment Gari half expected to get the woman's beer bottle smashed across her face. The woman had picked the right soundtrack for it, so perhaps that was her mood. But Gari didn't flinch and the woman's expression softened.

"Can't I be both, city girl?"

"How do you know I'm from the cities?"

"You're not the only one who can read a person, sister."

"So, you are a lesbian?"

The woman took a swig of beer. "I'm just a gal who likes to have fun."

Before Gari could say anything more, she felt a hand clamp on her shoulder, fingertips digging under her clavicle. The hand spun her around to face a monster of a man. Tobacco spit ran down his beard – redneck rabies. His anger gave way to surprise. Perhaps he expected to see a man's face, due to Gari's short hair. Then the anger came back. "What are you saying to my lady?"

Gari glanced back at the woman in the overalls. The woman winked and it seemed like the volume went up on her jukebox fight song. So the woman didn't want to get into a fight. She just wanted to see one. That's when Gari's whiskey kicked in.

"All the sweet things you forgot to tell her." She inched closer to the man, who was at least a foot taller. Then she added the phrase she'd seen start more bar fights than any other. "Got a problem with that?"

The ox didn't hesitate. There would be no "I'm not going to fight a girl" nonsense tonight. He swung, a wild haymaker that had no chance of landing with her standing so close. She ducked it and on her way up kneed him in the crotch.

The blow sent him reeling backward where a random man cracked an ashtray over his head, a white knight who probably thought a fight between a woman who had grown up brawling with four brothers and a drunken ox who could barely stand was somehow unfair for the woman.

With that, the bar erupted into a melee.

Gari turned back to the woman in the coveralls, who sipped her beer and smirked.

The woman asked, "You wanna get out of here, brawler?

Gari followed the woman as she weaved through combatants and out the back door. Outside, a few flakes of snow got caught in the glare of the backdoor light. "You planned that."

"And you knew it."

"I did."

"Yet you still went along with my plan."

"Yep."

"So you're fully aware you're getting into trouble."

Gari nodded. The woman in the overalls took her hand and led her to the far edge of the parking lot, to a beat up black cargo van. The snow picked up, melting on Gari's warm cheeks.

The woman in the overalls opened the back doors. The scent of straw wafted out. Bales were packed tight inside, up to the ceiling, but in the center they were only stacked one bale deep, leaving a little tunnel. "Climb in, city girl."

Gari did as ordered. She crawled in on hands and knees. Before she could turn over, she heard the doors slam shut. The woman's body pressed against her backside, warm breath on her neck. The woman tugged on Gari's blaze orange jacket. "Take this off."

Gari lay on her back and wiggled out of the jacket. Straw poked into her ears, snuck into the gap between her jeans and her sweatshirt, found its way up her pant leg to tickle her ankles. The woman slid Gari's shirt off, undid Gari's bra. The woman kissed her, hard. She grabbed Gari's wrists and pressed them down so forcefully she buried them in the straw. The woman's strength caught Gari off guard. She'd never been with a woman stronger than herself. She wasn't sure she liked it.

The woman released her grip, unbuttoned her overall straps and removed her top. Gari longed to see the woman's muscles, but what sparse glow made it through the van's windshield was caught by the straw bales, leaving only random slices of light to spotlight a nipple here, a patch of ribcage there - enough to let Gari know this woman had been hiding something spectacular under her overalls.

The woman leaned in again, pressing her skin against Gari's. Gari unzipped her pants, caught the woman's hand

and shoved it inside her panties. The woman kissed Gari all over the face, forehead, eyeballs, cheeks, wherever. Gari didn't like it, so she put both hands around the woman's head, wove her fingers together at the base of her neck and pulled her in toward her mouth only.

The van shook suddenly. Fists pounded on the exterior. Gari found her sweatshirt and threw it back on. "Is this your man?" she asked.

"He wasn't my man. He wouldn't know this is my van."

Gari almost wished it was. She could handle him. She didn't know if she could handle whatever random homophobic hicks were about to drag her and her new friend out into the snowy parking lot. She'd dealt with harassment before, but not often. That was in Minneapolis though. This was the woods of Wisconsin. Who knew what these rednecks would do?

The blows against the side of the van escalated. The men outside howled. They pushed the van, trying to tip it over. Gari searched the darkness for a weapon, but only found straw. Perhaps she could use one of the bales to plow over whoever was out there.

Suddenly the howling turned to a familiar laughter.

The passenger door opened and Daniel popped his head in. "No hanky panky!"

Gari screamed. "Chuck, get your ugly cronies out of here!"

Her brother could barely speak through his laughter. "I couldn't stop them."

"You know these twerps?" the woman in the overalls asked.

Todd opened the driver's side door and gazed in. "Who you calling twerps?"

The woman hurtled over Gari to the front of the van. She grabbed Todd's skull with both hands and threw him out while simultaneously evicting Daniel with a kick to the sternum. She closed the doors again while the boys cracked up outside.

"Sorry," Gari said.

"It's fine." The woman slid into the driver's seat and Gari finally got a look at her body in the light flooding in through the windshield. She'd never seen such a ripped woman. So in awe of the woman's physique, Gari barely registered the key turning in the ignition.

"I actually should stay here," Gari protested. "I'm with those guys, unfortunately."

"You seriously want to stay with them instead of coming with me?" The woman continued driving. The van was out of the parking lot now and on the road.

"I don't want to, but…"

"Oh shut up." The woman's tone lost all pretense of playfulness.

The van moved fast now. Gari saw the speedometer pass sixty. She crawled carefully over the bales of straw to the passenger seat, where she buckled her seatbelt. Her heart raced, and she wasn't sure it was because of the foreplay or the kidnapping. That's what this was, she told herself. She was being kidnapped. But it was hard for her to think of it that way because the woman was still topless as she drove the van, eyes locked onto the country highway ahead of them.

Topless or not, the woman's silence scared Gari. She'd had some interesting rendezvous with women since she realized she was gay as a teen, some clandestine and awkward meetings, but nothing like this. This was a bit more intense than she could deal with, and the way the woman's expression stayed neutral and she didn't take her gaze from the road wasn't helping either.

"Are you going to tell me where we're going at least?" Gari asked.

"Where nobody can find us," she answered. Still expressionless. Still immobile.

"We're in the middle of nowhere Wisconsin. You just described everywhere."

Finally the woman smiled again and relief filled Gari. She relaxed into her seat, turned on the cassette player. More country music. Waylon. "Lonesome, O'nry and Mean." The chugging bass took the wheel and pushed the van faster. Fresh snow swirled on the blacktop, teasing at hiding the road, making it a puzzle that blended with the white accumulating along the ditch.

Gari clutched the sides of her seat as the woman spun the wheel hard, taking the van off the road. If there was a driveway, Gari couldn't see it under the snow.

A barn appeared in the van's headlights, an old one, with all but the faintest flecks of red beaten away by time. The woman pulled up close. She left the van running, jumped out and wrestled the barn door open. The door's wheels groaned across the rusty rail.

The woman turned the headlights off and pulled the van into the barn.

"I can't see anything," Gari said.

The woman stepped out of the van again. She closed the barn door, sealing them in total darkness. Opening the passenger door, she took Gari's hands and helped her out. "You're scared."

"No."

"Why not?"

Gari didn't know how to respond. She couldn't see the woman's face to read her expression. This didn't feel playful anymore. This didn't feel sexy. She considered insisting that the woman take her back to Jack's, but she had a feeling the woman would say no, and she didn't want to hear the woman say no. So she let the woman lead her by the hand further into the shadows.

Darkness this intense didn't exist in Minneapolis. Too much artificial light. Even in the basement of her house with the lights off, streetlights edged in through the glass brick windows, making it easy to navigate around the washer and dryer, the archery targets she stored in the winter.

Though she couldn't see anything, she sensed that the barn wasn't empty. The woman didn't guide her in a straight line. She weaved through the darkness, moving around things, perhaps dodging broken down tractors. Gari heard animal noises, breathing. Maybe there were a dairy cows tucked away in the dark, sleeping. Or it could have been her own breath, which Gari suddenly realized was very loud.

The woman's lips touched Gari's briefly before she shoved her backwards. Gari screamed, but her scream turned to laughter when she fell into another bale of straw. Her eyes started to adjust to the darkness and she saw the outline of the woman in overalls above her. The moonlight squeezing through the slats of wood formed thin bars on Gari's skin, on the bales of hay around her.

As the woman leaned in for another kiss, Gari noticed something further back, other outlines in the moonlight. They looked like people, not moving, just standing there. "What the…."

The woman snapped at Gari's throat.

Gari grabbed the woman's hair with both hands and pulled her away, but not before the woman's teeth scratched Gari's neck. Blood drizzled from the wound, channeling down Gari's chest.

She shoved the woman aside and ran. The woman snagged the back of Gari's sweatshirt, but Gari fell forward with all her weight and broke free, diving into the shadows of the barn, sprinting frantically. Her shin collided with something cold and metal, sending her flying forward. Her face hit the barn wall and she fell, wedged between the wall of the barn and whatever she'd tripped over. Flailing her arms to get a grip on something to pull herself up, she caught what felt like a heavy cloth hanging from the wall. She used it to climb back onto her feet.

"Come, come," the woman called. "Where's my brawler?"

Gari pressed her back against the wall and froze. She gazed around, squinting as if closing her eyelids till they were razor thin would let her cut through the darkness. She looked up and realized that the heavy cloth wasn't only covering the barn wall, but a window. If she could tug it down, she might illuminate the barn enough to see a way out, or at least see what was happening.

As quietly as possible, she grabbed the cloth and pulled. It held in place. Frantically, she yanked and yanked, giving up on silence. Soon the top corner fell loose, unleashing a cloud of dust that glimmered in the swath of moonlight that gouged through the window.

Gari had been right. There were other people in the barn, dozens of them. They weren't moving though, might not have even been alive. Naked, they dangled from fleshy tubes driven into the tops of their skulls, their feet inches from the cold dirt floor of the barn. The tubes looked bruised and gnawed. They throbbed, a pumping motion.

Gari followed one of the tubes from where it began, atop a flesh-peeled face, up high into the barn, where it twisted around uneven rafters, running toward a high corner before dropping back to the ground to meet all the others in the corner. There, something sat that Gari couldn't comprehend.

A mass of pale flesh, as if several humans had been melted down and smeared into the corner, a bad caulk job meant to plug the holes in the barn. Gutters of skin and gangrenous muscle entwined with cobwebs and dotted with bat feces. A massive mouth gaped, ringed with broken teeth that clamped onto the tubes that converged there. The fleshy body pulsed as it sucked from the tubes.

The woman, her overalls down, breasts soaked in moonlight, sauntered toward the thing in the corner, sitting on a shelf of meat that might have been called a lap. Daintily, with pinkies extended, she lifted one of the tubes from the creature's maw and put it to her own lips. She drank deep. Thick liquid poured down her chin, globs of pink and yellow muck, the liquified insides of whichever person hung at the other end of the tube.

Sated, the woman took the tube from her mouth, held it out in offering to Gari. "Want some?"

Gari ran, leaping over heaps of rusty chickenwire, weaving through the bodies that hung like garish ornaments. The moonlight illuminated the van, revealing that what had felt impossibly far in the darkness was so close. She climbed in and frantically locked the doors.

She flipped down the visors and dug through the glove compartment in search of the key. The topless woman circled the van, stood in front of it. She opened her mouth wide, so wide the corners of her lips cracked open. She grinned at Gari with massive fangs.

Gari screamed and instinctively reached for the ignition. The keys had been there all along. She turned the van on, shifted into reverse and hit the gas, crashing into the barn door so hard it flung off the rail and landed ten feet away with a thud. Snow came down harder now, hiding the path they had taken to the barn. Gari drove anyway, dodging trees and shrubs.

She made it to blacktop. She didn't know where she was, but that barn and the horrors within were behind her. It didn't feel behind her though. The image of that creature in the corner clung to her. The smell. How had she not noticed it as soon as she stepped into the barn? Rot and waste so pungent it stuck to her clothes. Had she stepped in it? Had she run through puddles of death dissolved under those hanging bodies? The thought of it stuck to her boots made her nauseous.

Despite her shaking knees, she pushed harder on the gas. Her headlights shined across a sign for County Highway D. That's where the cabin was. She remembered that. She could remember the rest of the way. Barely decelerating, she slid through the turn.

Something thumped on the top of the van. Hail. The snow must have turned to hail. Wisconsin weather could get weird at this time of year, so it wasn't unusual. More thumps. But she didn't see any hail on the road in front of her, just growing drifts of snow.

She rounded a bend that looked familiar and there was another thump, a loud one, as if something had landed atop the van. "That's not possible," she whispered. Her mind was playing tricks on her. She'd been through something terrible and now her brain was giving her false signals, turning the noises an old van made into threats. She reminded herself that neither the woman nor the thing in the corner could have followed her. She was safe.

But then two hands reached down in front of the windshield. Long claws slashed at the wipers, breaking them off. Then the hands disappeared. Next, a crunching sound, as if something launched off the top of the van. Had it left, whatever it was? She flashed back to the topless woman's razor smile, dripping liquified organs. But it couldn't be her. How could she have kept up with the van? Whatever it was, it was gone now. Gari didn't hear anymore sounds on top of the van.

Snow accumulated quickly on the windshield without the wipers to knock it away. Gari refused to stop, to give whatever was out there the chance to hurt her. Keeping her eyes on the road and one hand on the wheel, she reached the other frantically around the van. She found a long-handled snow scraper behind the passenger seat. Maintaining her speed, she rolled down her window enough to reach out with the scraper, clearing her windshield enough to see the carved wooden eagle that marked the gravel driveway to the cabin.

Her relief was short lived. Something slashed her hand, forcing her to drop the scraper and roll up the window. The blood on the back of her hand gleamed in the moonlight. She was bleeding from her hand and her neck now, from the bite earlier. She'd almost forgotten about the bite. Just a scratch really, almost playful, but enough to draw blood. She felt the wound. The blood had crusted at the edges. She nervously chipped away at the crust as she turned into the gravel drive.

Firelight oozed through the cabin windows and she could feel its warmth as she stopped the van. The boys were there. They wouldn't believe her, but they were there. For a moment she wondered if she shouldn't have come here. Had she led whatever that thing was here? Would it hurt her brother? The other men? She didn't think any of them would be of much value in a fight, except Big Chuck. No sense in worrying about it now. She was here. And her weapon was inside.

With a deep breath she flung open the van door and ran to the cabin. She swore she could hear wings flapping around her. Laughter. That was definitely laughter coming from somewhere above. She plowed through the door and slammed it behind her.

She barely had time to register the boys' "I know what you were up to" smirks fall away as they saw the blood on her neck, her hand. Gari went straight for her bow. She pulled it out of its case and strapped her quiver of arrows onto her back.

As she nocked an arrow, one of the men finally spoke. Her brother. "Are you okay?"

"Open the door," she screamed, drawing the bowstring, feeling the tension run through her, feeling her body turn into a weapon.

"What's going on, Gari?" Her brother asked. He and the other men sat stunned. Only Big Chuck moved. He opened the door, nodded at her as she stepped out into the blowing snow.

As ice thickened on her eyelashes, she kneeled down near the van, weapon ready. The flapping was distant at first, then grew louder, closer. She sighted the patch of night sky where the sound came from, but saw nothing but white flakes erupting from the darkness, scintillating in the moonlight.

Keep breathing, she told herself. The flapping sounded like it was on top of her now. Panic flashed through her. Maybe the sound was bouncing around the woods, throwing her off. Maybe that thing was behind her. Maybe it was on top of her now.

She fought her thoughts away. She had to trust her senses. The flapping was coming from in front of her, louder and louder, filling her ears, matching her heartbeat. Still she saw nothing.

Then eyes, glowing green, emerging through the barrage of snow. Massive black wings beat the sky around them. The woman. So much different now. Some sort of creature, diving straight at Gari from the darkness. She smiled as she dove, not threatened in the least by Gari's weapon. Everything in Gari told her to run, but where would she go?

She tightened her draw, sighted the woman's bare chest. If there was a heart there, Gari was going to send an arrow straight through it. The winged creature cackled, coming closer and closer.

Gari breathed. Her first hunt would be a success.

She released the arrow.

A CENTAURESS WALKS INTO
A BATTLE

"POUR ME SOMETHING THAT BURNS," THE CENTAURESS TOLD the barmaid with a wink as a bearded beast of a man scraped his barstool across the packed dirt floor to sidle up beside her.

"A woman like you shouldn't be alone in a place like this." He blew the words through his bristles like spitting seeds, carrying the stink of rotting teeth with them.

Even if his eyes weren't fuzzy with drink, he couldn't have seen the set of her jaw through the smears of color she had painted on for this rare night out, nor the striations of her sleek muscles through the silken pink ruffles of finery that covered her torso and cascaded down her back, over the spot where human turned to horse, over her four rigid legs with their hooves planted firmly, steadily on the ground.

She grinned. "I suppose you will protect me?"

"Ask any man at this mangy inn and he will tell you there is no greater warrior in the land." He gestured grandly toward the drunken, disinterested patrons. "I've been battling since birth."

As a filly, she had followed her mother and father into battle. This was their life, and the life of the generations that had preceded them. It would be hers as well. They taught her to swing a sword, always for results, never for show. At great cost, they demonstrated the mistakes not to make, leaving pieces of themselves on the battlefield in the process. Until one day, there was no more of them left to walk away and she stood on the battlefield alone, a mare now, head held high, her muscles painted with the blood of her enemy.

The man slapped his formidable bicep with his opposite hand to emphasize the pink lines that crisscrossed it. "My scars tell all that need be told."

"I see."

To her, scars were nothing to brag about, a symbol of one's inability to defend oneself. Her skin remained pristine, untouched by blade. No cudgel had damaged her fur. She had no marks save for those on her hocks from charging too quickly into battle over jagged rocks or through bramble. They had only recently healed from her last fight, when she had nearly broken all four of her legs by hurling herself off a cliff to position herself in the middle of the fray. She had landed awkwardly on rough terrain, but recovered confidently with sword drawn, much to her enemy's slit-throat surprise.

"I have fought in many battles in my time," he said, tugging at his beard with gnarled fingers. "Hundreds of battles."

"Oh!" she said. The bartender slid a goblet of brown muck in front of her and she finished it in a single sip.

She had fought in fourteen battles. Granted, she was younger than this man, but she was certain those fourteen were all that had occurred in her lifetime within the radius her hooves could carry her. She had also been in thirty-three skirmishes, forty-nine one-on-ones and had once been ambushed by a sorceress with a trained bear. That one had been dicey, as she had never dealt with magic before and a whispered spell turned her horse body to stone temporarily. Thankfully, the bear had much greater allegiance to the half of a roasted pig the centauress carried in her sack than to the sorceress.

"I've broken blades over the skulls of marauders," the man continued, sipping carefully from his own mug for fear of spilling into the thickets of his beard.

She had left a sword behind only once, after slicing it deep into the craggy cheek of a festering cave troll, who took offense at the gesture and attempted to mash her underfoot. She had easily dodged his stomps. In his anger, he had neglected the cliff she guided him toward, and he stumbled over the edge, taking her blade with him. She had loved that sword. She still mourned for that sword.

"If anyone here so much as looks at you in an untoward manner…" He trailed off, tapping a forefinger on the pommel of the battle axe he dragged alongside him.

She gazed at the man's fingers as they grasped the axe handle. They were thick, with sprouts of black hair twisting from gashes and spots of dry skin, not weak by any means. Sometimes, for fleeting moments, on the darkest of nights, she forgot her strength and longed to feel safe, to feel protected. If only that was something as easy to find as a cocky man with a battle axe. But then the sun would rise, and she would stretch her arms to the sky and dig her hooves in deep beside a battlefield red with her enemy's blood, feeling ashamed for wanting anything more than her own strength to see her through.

"I like you, woman of few words."

The man bought more rounds and told more tales. The two of them tapped their goblets together 'til dawn, when he finally crumpled drunk to the floor, squeezing his battle axe against his chest like a toy.

The centauress drained her last drink and gazed down at the mightiest warrior in all the land, now drooling a puddle around her black hooves. She stepped over him with her powerful horse legs and walked out into the waiting, ever-warring world she called home.

DROWNER

HE STARTED SCREAMING FOR HELP BEFORE HE EVEN TOUCHED the water.

I was sitting beside the icy lake, by myself, trying to get my head straight. When he popped out of the woods on the opposite side, I went still, hoping he wouldn't notice me. I wanted to be alone. That's why I came out here on a see-your-breath day. But he saw me anyway. When he did, he got frantic.

"Help," he cried, his voice breaking as he ran into the lake. He screamed and splashed until he was knee deep, looking at me. Did he expect me to swim over there? To run around the lake for him? I didn't move, and he retreated to shore.

He kept screaming though, running along the shoreline, closing the space between us. Occasionally, he would dive back into the water, making his way in until he was waist deep, before realizing I wasn't going to come to his rescue. Then he'd drag his drenched body onto land once again.

I sat quietly on my little cliff a few feet above the lake, hoping he wouldn't keep coming around. I needed space for my thoughts. I had things I needed to piece together, a life to reassess.

What did he want anyway? To make me think he was drowning? To get me to try to save him? What would he do if I did? Try to pull me under?

As he got closer and his splashing became wilder, I was certain I noticed spears of malice coming out of his eyes. I had seen this look before from men with their thumbs up alongside the highway, and in the faces of those who walked away from me. How many people had he drowned this way? Well, I was not going to be next. I would not play this ridiculous game.

Neck deep, he waved his arms and bellowed, "Help! Please!" Two words. Just those two words over and over. He went under and then came up, spitting lake water and screaming some more. The act was convincing, almost hypnotic. I felt my weight shifting, as if to stand. He saw it too and almost broke character to smile. Almost. I stayed put, and he eventually made his way back to shore, never losing eye contact with me for more than a second.

He kept moving along the shore, getting closer to where I sat. It wasn't a big lake. I wished it was. Why didn't he just quit? Couldn't he see I wasn't falling for it?

I opened my mouth to ask what he was doing, but bit back the question. His answer could ensnare me. I refused to give him the opportunity to pull me in with his words. I would sit still and this would pass. Everything would pass.

Soon he reached a point where he couldn't continue along shore. It was all trees and rock face. That's why I had picked this spot. No chance of someone casually coming by walking a dog or strolling hand-in-hand with a lover. For a moment, it looked like he might give up. His screaming slowed.

Then he dove into the lake and swam, actually swam, straight for me. He had to skirt spots that had already iced over. I couldn't imagine how cold the water was. Shivers broke his screams for help, even as he swam confidently toward me.

Ten feet away, he stopped swimming and flailed his arms, bobbing under occasionally, begging for help whenever he popped back up. I stayed still and he paddled closer. The chattering of his teeth punctuated his screams.

I couldn't tell when his act faded in favor of real panic, but it must have at some point, perhaps when he realized how deep the lake was on this side, even this close to shore. But he wasn't close to shore now, not really. The precipice I sat on wasn't high, but high enough to be insurmountable from the water.

The man splashed and screamed. "Help! Please!"

He reached his arm out toward me.

I didn't take it.

I sat still.

"Help! Please!" Two words. Two more words.

His skin started to go blue, his blood slowing under the influence of the icy water. Still, he kept his arm raised toward me, even when his legs were too frozen to kick, even when he sank under, even when he stopped coming back up.

I didn't take it.

LOVE SKULL

In that catacomb, one skull stood out from thousands. While the others had let time and rot strip them of their humanity, becoming nothing more than putrescent decorations on the sepulchral walls, this one still expressed life. It was just as fleshless, just as yellowed as the rest. Its eye sockets were no less hollow, but somewhere in those ocular shadows danced the faintest hint of longing. Perhaps this one had died staring into the eyes of its true love. No, for that would have been a gentle death, and this one had not died gently. Scars and fissures crisscrossed its forehead. Its left cheekbone had been destroyed, so the shadows from that eye socket dripped down like dark tears.

DEON READ THIS PASSAGE IN CORBY BENTON'S EIGHTIES horror hit *Night Skulls* and stopped. He reread it. Gorgeous. He loved the paragraph and he loved that skull. He could picture it perfectly in his mind. He closed the book for a moment and gazed around the bathroom stall, but the image of the skull remained locked in his brain.

He flipped to the passage and read it again, spending time with every word, every detail. When he reached the end of the paragraph, he couldn't move on. He had to go back and read it again, as if doing so would allow him to unlock new sentences, new information about that skull.

He had never been a Benton fan, but he found the man's books easy, mindless reading to fill the long gaps between calls at the call center where he worked third shift. And on bathroom breaks. Usually, he could pick them up and put them down, but this passage wasn't the usual Benton hackery. This passage required Deon's undivided attention.

Giggling, he ripped the page out of the book. Page five hundred and seventy-nine. Everything that had come before that paragraph had been trash. Everything after it would likely be too. He threw the rest of the mass-market paperback into the puddle behind the toilet. Then he read the paragraph again.

And again.

And again.

Until his legs grew numb and he knew his coworkers would be wondering what was taking him so long. He folded the page, stashed it in his back pocket and reached for the toilet paper. When he looked up, the skull was there, floating in front of him.

He recoiled. In his panic, he almost screamed.

Regaining control, he told himself that the skull was merely in his mind, vivid from so many readings. But he couldn't blink the skull away. It stared at him, beautiful and battered, its sockets filled with shadows and longing. Without thinking, he reached out slowly with his pointer finger and gently touched the tip of the skull's nasal bone. Solid. Bone solid.

"Hello?" Deon said.

"Hello, my love," the skull replied in a sweet, androgynous voice that whistled ever so slightly as it swept through a mouth of missing teeth.

Suddenly self-conscious, Deon reached under the skull

and grabbed a wad of toilet paper, quickly wiping himself. When he stood and pulled up his pants, the skull floated up with him, remaining at eye level. It circled Deon's head once before returning to stare into Deon's eyes. There it floated, almost perfectly still except for a little wobble now and then. Deon waved his hand above the skull, checking for a string. When he didn't find one, he wondered if the bathroom had recently been cleaned, if he had maybe accidentally huffed some toxic fumes. Or maybe working overnight shifts was finally getting the best of him.

"You're the skull from the book?" he asked.

"I've been read so many times, but it never felt like this before. I could feel the love pouring out of your eyes and into the page, into the words, into me."

"I should get back to work now," he said, confident he was hallucinating.

"Okay, my love."

Instead of running straight out of the bathroom, he acted rationally. He washed up and looked in the mirror, running his hands over his blonde buzz cut and adjusting the collar of his work-supplied orange polo shirt. He looked fine. He looked perfectly normal. Except for the skull floating over his left shoulder like a second head. But it wasn't there. It couldn't possibly be.

He stepped out of the bathroom and was greeted with a scream. Gary, the third-shift supervisor, was looking straight at Deon, or rather, at the spot above Deon's shoulder where the skull floated. The old man had his hands on the sides of his face and was giving the most ridiculous, wide-eyed, high-pitched scream Deon had ever heard. Deon almost laughed, thinking this was part of the hallucination, but then other coworkers appeared, drawn to the ruckus, and they too screamed.

The skull floated behind Deon's head, attempting to hide.

Not knowing what else to do, Deon feigned checking his fly and asked dumbly, "What's wrong? What's going on?"

Joe Beth, Deon's cube mate and sometimes late-night hand-job provider, grabbed for the skull. As the skull flitted out of her reach, keeping Deon's head between it and her tender, clutching fingers, she said, "There's a damn skull floating around your head, Dee. What the fuck!"

So he was not hallucinating.

"It's no big deal." He shrugged.

Joe Beth continued her attempt to snatch the skull from its orbit. "Oh, okay. I guess it's one of those no-big-deal floating skulls, huh?"

"Basically."

As the screams died out, Gary, with a raspy voice, ordered everyone back to their cubicles to take phone calls. Joe Beth seemed reluctant to give up without having caught her prey, but finally sighed, slapped Deon on the ass and swaggered back to their shared cube.

Deon started to follow, but Gary called him back.

"Uh, are you feeling sick?" Gary asked.

"No."

Gary looked at the ground. "Would you like to go home?"

"I've only been here three hours."

"Don't you want to go home and…" he pointed at the skull, "…figure that out?"

"I need the hours."

"Deon, you're fired!" Gary shouted. As he walked away, he mumbled, "And if HR wants to get on my case about skull discrimination, they can kiss my ass."

Deon figured it wasn't worth arguing about. He cleaned out his cubicle, with Joe Beth giving him the pouty lip routine, as if he had done this just to evade her handjobs. Truth be told, he wasn't going to miss those handjobs. They were the least sexy sex acts he had ever engaged in. She had even said once, "It's more like steering a car than having sex, which is why I don't think I'm cheating on my boyfriend." He used that same logic to convince himself he wasn't cheating on his girlfriend. He was just getting his steering wheel steered.

Outside, the fall air felt nice, not too cool yet. Sweatshirt weather. He didn't mind walking home. It was only a couple miles. Usually, he took the bus, but usually he got done with work at six in the morning, not three. Walking was probably best in this situation anyway, all things considered.

As he walked through quiet, moonlit neighborhoods, the skull circled his head.

"Skull?" he asked.

"Yes, my love?" the skull replied.

"Could you stop that? You're making me dizzy."

The skull paused and hovered directly in front of him, staring back at him as he walked. This slowed him down at first, because he flinched with every step, fearing that his head would collide with the skull if he moved too quickly. However, the skull effortlessly kept a foot of space between them. This was actually more awkward than the circling, but Deon didn't bother to ask the skull to move. He had a more pressing question.

"Why do you call me, 'my love?'"

The skull inched closer and locked onto him with its shadowy sockets, more vision in their emptiness somehow than in most eyes Deon had stared into. He stopped walking, worried that one more step would send him falling into those dark, cavernous holes. He would drown in their longing.

Except the longing was gone now. It had been replaced by something else, something that made him much more uncomfortable.

The skull replied to Deon's question. "You have to ask?"

He nodded, not because he truly needed to ask, but because he needed the answer verbalized. He needed it in a more tangible form, and if that made it clunky, if that made it less romantic, then so be it.

"I felt your eyes. They looked me up and down, reading me from every angle, trying to discover more about me, about my history, a violent history that the author implied, but never bothered to write, so you will never know, I will never know. But that doesn't matter, because you read what was there, so lovingly, and now I am here, and I have a future. We have a future. Together."

Well, that certainly didn't make it any less romantic.

Deon considered arguing with the skull. He considered denying his love for the skull. He considered the old get-rid-of-the-clingy-puppy-for-its-own-good-by-telling-it-you-hate-it routine. None of that felt right though. The fucked up thing was that this skull hovering in front of his face, it felt right. So right.

Deon was not okay with how right it felt.

And neither was Tanya, his girlfriend. As soon as he stepped into the apartment they shared, she freaked out. She was sitting on the couch, smoking weed and eating whipped cream and watching sitcoms from the seventies, placid as hell, and then she turned and saw Deon and the skull and she seemed to instantly get unstoned. She hurled the little tub of whipped cream straight at Deon's face.

Valiantly, the skull swished in front of him, taking the hit. Whipped cream splattered into its eye sockets, up its nasal cavity. The tub slid to the ground and landed with a plop. Deon accidentally stepped in it as he moved toward Tanya to try to calm her down.

"Chill out, Tee," he said, calling her by her pet name, which he had given her mainly because it rhymed with his nickname. Tee and Dee. It sounded sweet.

Tanya attempted to flee, limbing onto the couch. "Don't tell me to chill out when there's a big fucking skull hovering around your head!"

"Big?" the skull asked.

"Like the fattest skull I have ever seen," Tanya clarified.

The skull heated up, boiling the whipped cream. The dessert topping bubbled and crackled, unnaturally white against the skull's yellowing bones,. It puddled on the floor beneath the skull like a hot, white shadow.

"Fatty, fatty skull bones, ruler of the gross zone!" Tanya taunted.

The skull opened its mouth wide, viciously baring its few remaining teeth.

Tanya screeched, "Keep it away from me!"

Ideally, Deon would have liked to let the two work out their differences themselves. He just wasn't into conflict. He didn't know what to do with it. Asking him to partake in or resolve any sort of argument was akin to asking him to do trigonometry or build a space engine or have an extended conversation with his grandma about her personal hygiene. But in this situation, like so many calls with Grams, he didn't see a way around it, so he pulled out his best argument stopper.

"Hey, let's all sit down and smoke a bowl, okay?"

The sound of sizzling whipped cream faded and he felt the skull cool. Tanya sat on the far side of the couch, crossing her arms awkwardly over her boobs. The girl was all boobs. Everything she ate went into her boobs, and then slowly strengthened the rest of her body for the sole purpose of supporting her boobs. Deon got kind of revved up when she crossed her arms over them, squishing them together, but at the moment he needed to focus on getting everyone settled down.

He sat next to Tanya. The skull floated to the opposite side of the couch. Seated between the woman he loved and the skull he loved, Deon started working with the pot on the coffee table, loading up the pipe.

Without thinking about it, he took the first hit. To be fair, he needed it the most. It had been a rough day. He lost his job. Maybe he should mention that to Tanya, to get some sympathy out of her before getting fully into the skull thing. Telling her was a gamble though, because she might get mad. They weren't exactly swimming in bank, and she had a bad habit of worrying about paying rent and shit.

He handed the pipe to Tanya and grabbed a book off the stack of grubby mass-market horror paperbacks next to the couch. He was going to use it as a prop to explain what had happened, but he inadvertently flipped it open and started reading a paragraph about a slimy swamp monster and then, seemingly of their own accord, his hands smashed the book shut and flung it across the room. The last thing he needed was a swamp monster lurking behind him 24/7.

"What the fuuuuuck?" Tanya asked, handing the pipe back to Deon.

He took another hit and shrugged. Then he held the pipe up to the skull's mouth. The skull inhaled, but all the smoke came out through its ear cracks, which Deon thought was hilarious. Tanya did too. They both cracked up and leaned into each other. The pot was good. They finished it off and fell asleep on the couch and didn't get around to the skull discussion.

At four in the afternoon, Deon woke alone on the couch. Well, not alone, because the skull was still there. Tanya was gone though. She had left a note on the coffee table. It said, "Off to work. Please get rid of skull."

Deon sighed, pried himself off the couch and poured a bowl of sugary cereal. He tended to do what Tanya wanted. It just made life easier. He got to come home and smoke pot and snuggle with her without conflict, and sure, sometimes that meant he had to do the dishes or run some stupid errand or skip a hangout night with his dude buds because she was feeling needy, but that rarely felt like a big sacrifice. This was different though. He kind of felt attached to this skull. Fully attached.

"Skull, what am I gonna do with you?"

"Love me."

He took a couple bites of cereal. "I do, but I love Tanya too."

The skull orbited his head as he finished his breakfast. He thought about taking a shower, but he was concerned about taking his shirt off without upsetting the skull. Sniffing his armpits, he decided there really was no need to change, since he had showered yesterday and he hadn't built up any stink he could detect over the lingering weed fumes. He ran his hands over his buzz cut and poked the sleep crud out of his eye crotches with his pinkies. Good to go.

"Hey skull, how come nobody else ever noticed you like I did?"

"I was buried in those catacombs. I was buried in a book that was nine hundred and eighty-nine pages long. I guess everybody scanned over me, one little detail amidst so much extraneous material."

"The whole book should have been about you."

"For you it was, and that's all that matters."

Deon poured himself another bowl of cereal, not because he was hungry, but because he needed something colorful to think over. He had this idea that the bowl full of multicolored Os would help him focus.

His preferred solution would be to figure out a way to keep the skull and Tanya. He loved Tanya. She made him comfortable. He would go so far as to say he would fight someone over Tanya. Once, when they were grocery shopping, the line was really long and Tanya was waiting patiently when some grizzled old dude cut in front of her. Deon put his hand on the man's shoulder and said, "The lady was here first." He made a little fist, but kept it down by his side. The man must have felt Deon's fist-clench radiate through the air, because the old dude shrugged and stepped behind Tanya.

Deon didn't know if he'd do the same for the skull, but that didn't seem like what this relationship was about. It was the skull that made him feel safe. It had blocked that tub of whipped cream from hitting Deon in the face. Sure, it was just whipped cream, but if the skull hadn't blocked it, Deon definitely would have had to shower today.

Deon's phone buzzed. A text from Tanya: "Is skull gone?"

Deon texted back: "Working on it."

And then, as if it rode into his brain on the scent of artificial fruit flavor that wafted up from his cereal bowl, he had his solution.

"Skull, I just thought of something."

"What, my love?"

"Don't you need to get back in the book?"

"Nobody cares," the skull replied.

"Well, nobody cares like I do. But still, you really set the mood in that catacombs scene. I didn't finish the book or anything, but I'm sure it's not the same without you." He could not let this go. He needed to show the skull that it was necessary to return back home to the pages of Night Skulls. He tossed the bowl of cereal in the sink and rushed for the door, the skull orbiting him as he hustled on foot to the musty used bookstore a few blocks from the apartment.

Inside, he went straight for the horror section, crossing his fingers that they would have a copy of Night Skulls. He had never been to a used bookstore that didn't have at least a dozen Corby Benton books for sale, and Night Skulls was one of the most popular, so it wasn't a long shot. Sure enough, the store had three copies, each with a perfectly busted spine and yellowing pages.

Deon flipped one open to page five hundred and seventy-nine. He couldn't believe what he saw. He refused to believe it. Throwing that copy on the ground, he grabbed the second

one, looked at that and found the same thing. Then he threw
that one on the ground too and picked up the third. Sure
enough, it was there too.

He read the paragraph out loud:

*In that catacomb, one beach ball stood out from thousands. While the
others had let time dull their red and yellow and green stripes, this one
still shined vibrantly. Despite sitting in the dust and dirt, it looked like it
had only recently been used by a gaggle of beach brats. It still reeked of
ocean salt.*

"This is ridiculous!" Deon screamed.

He marched to the front of the store to ask the bespecta-
cled clerk if she had ever read the book and if she remembered the skull scene, but she shrieked as soon as she saw the
skull, so he ran out of the store before he could ask. She was
probably more of a lit fan anyway.

Night fell and he walked around aimlessly.

He told the skull, "That book is stupid without you. It's
stupider without you."

"It's not classic literature. Nobody cares if it's a beach ball
or a skull."

"I care!"

"Yes, my love, and you're the only one, which is why I'm
here, with the one who cares about me the most, and who I
care about so much."

Deon sighed. He and the skull were definitely attached.

There was only one other logical way to shake the skull.
He had to show the skull how much harm it would do him if
he kept it around. Surely the skull didn't want to harm him,
even if it didn't seem to care if he lost Tanya.

"Skull, I don't think I'm going to be able to get a new job
with you around."

"As long as we're together," the skull said.

"I can't pay rent and buy food on togetherness."

"I think you'll get a job. I believe in you, my love."

He would have to show the skull. It was nearly eleven and his legs were tired, but surely there was someplace he could stop into and get an application, or maybe even an interview. It would have to be someplace chill. On the off chance that he actually did get the job, he didn't want it to be a grind. The call center was kind of a grind at the start and end of his shift, but in-between was mostly just hanging out and reading and getting under-the-desk handjobs.

He noticed the scrap yard on the other side of the street. There was a help wanted sign hanging from the closed gate. Night security guard, it read. "Whoa!" he said, thinking he might have discovered his dream job. He wanted a job where he could sit around all night. That's what night security guards did, right? He fantasized about lounging in front of a wall of screens that showed video feed from each of the aisles, feet up on his desk as he burned through one scummy horror paperback after the next. All night long. And then maybe there'd be a girl who would give him handjobs.

Caught up in this fantasy, he tripped on a crack in the sidewalk and fell down.

"Are you okay?" the skull asked, voice filled with concern.

He looked at his skinned knees. Blood seeped out, soaking into the edges of his newly torn jeans. "Oh, I really liked these pants!"

Maybe he wouldn't make a great night security guard.

But he decided, fuck it.

If he didn't get the job, it would prove to the skull that their relationship was doomed. And if he did get the job, that would be one less thing for Tanya to be mad about.

He crossed the street and tried to pull the gate open, but it was locked. After looking for a buzzer, he decided just to bang on it. No response. They definitely needed a night security guard. Maybe they had one, and he was sleeping. Deon could just scale the chain-ink fence and climb in. He didn't see any dogs. With a running start, he leaped onto the fence. It clanged loudly against the metal fence posts. He climbed up and jumped over, bellyflopping on the dirt inside the fence.

"This is fun, my love," the skull said.

Deon stood and looked around. In the dark, he couldn't see where the office was. All he could see was junk. Beat-up cars covered the terrain as far as the eye could see. Refrigerators. Stoves. Furnaces. Old style big screen TVs. Everything was dirty. He felt like a kid in a really big sandbox.

"Hello I'm here for a job application!" he shouted.

Noise rang out from behind a stack of cars.

Deon squinted in that direction. He walked toward the sound.

"Hello?" he asked.

He heard some mumbling, then three dudes appeared with a little red wagon full of windows and other parts. They pointed flashlights in his eyes.

"You guys are stealing stuff, aren't you?" he asked.

In lieu of an answer, one of the dudes charged him and knocked him to the ground. He closed his eyes. They surrounded him and kicked him in the ribs. It hurt pretty bad. He thought maybe he should play dead, but he didn't think they'd buy it and it was hard not to scream at least a little bit.

But then they started screaming too.

Deon opened his eyes. The skull, his beloved skull, had broken its orbit around his head. It opened its jaws wide. It opened its jaws wider than it should have. Its bones seemed to turn into rubber, allowing it to open its mouth wide enough to engulf one of the guy's heads completely. The skull bit the dude's head off like a kid who had never eaten a sucker before and didn't know that you're supposed to suck on it .

The dude's body remained on its feet for a surprisingly long time. Blood spurted out of his neck in a stream so thick it looked like a new, wet, red limb reaching into the sky to recover the head that had been stolen away.

The skull did not give the head back. It did not spit the head out. It chewed a couple times and swallowed it into whatever void hid at the back of its mouth.

Of the two remaining dudes, one ran. The other froze. The skull headbutted him so hard that the man's face flattened and his eyeballs popped out of their sockets. Still attached by ocular cords, each eyeball shot to an opposite side of the attacking skull. When they reached the ends of their tethers, they wrapped around the skull like a pair of arms giving it a welcoming hug.

The skull shook them off and flew after the other man.

Deon pulled himself to his feet. As he checked for broken bones, a couple other guys approached – an older gentleman and a uniformed guard.

A beach ball orbited the guard's head.

Eyeing the beach ball, Deon gave the uniformed man an understanding nod,.

"What's going on here?" the older gentleman asked.

"Ummm, these two dudes tried to rob you." Deon pointed at the massacred corpses. At that moment, the skull returned, dragging the third burglar by his foot. This man now wore his intestines like a scarf. Deon added, "And this guy."

"You stopped them?" the older gentleman asked. "While my paid security guard was fucking around with his beach ball?"

"Yeah, me and my, uh, skull."

"But why were you here? Were you trying to rob me too?"

Deon stood taller. "I'm here to inquire about your help wanted sign."

The older gentleman turned to the guard. He didn't say anything. Neither did the guard. The uniformed man just shrugged, took off his guard shirt, threw it on the ground and stomped toward the exit, beach ball floating lazily behind.

"How do you feel about being a night security guard?" the older gentleman asked. "You and your skull."

"Hell yeah," Deon replied.

He followed the older gentleman to an office, where he filled out some paperwork. The older gentleman, the owner of the junkyard, asked Deon to start immediately. Deon said he had some business to take care of, but he could start the following night. The owner agreed, and Deon practically ran home, excited about the new job. On the way though, he remembered his dilemma. He definitely couldn't get rid of the skull now, but he didn't know if Tanya would understand.

When he got home, he got a text from her: "I'm on my way home. Skull better be gone, or I will be." She definitely wouldn't understand.

The truth was he didn't want to get rid of the skull, and not just because of the new job either. The skull loved him. And it wasn't unrequited. Quite the contrary. He loved the skull. Not like a boy-girl love or even a familial love, but a strong love nonetheless, strong enough to lift the skull from the pages of Corby Benton's shitty book, that was for sure. He couldn't make the skull go away, any more than he could make his love for it go away. But he loved Tee too.

Another text from Tanya: "Looking forward to a skull-free night."

The skull orbited his head in silence.

He couldn't remember ever feeling this much pressure in his entire life. He thought about the baggie of pot awaiting him on the coffee table back home, promising a refuge from the pressure, but admitting it had no answers. He didn't know what to do. He could not let Tanya go. If only she could see the skull the way he saw the skull. If only the skull could be a part of her life like it had become a part of his life.

That was it. That was what he needed to do.

He scurried around the apartment, finding a pen and paper.

He needed to write Tanya a love letter, a very specific love letter, a love letter that would make her understand everything, make her see the skull like he did, make her love the skull like he did. And make the skull love her too. One letter to form the perfect love triangle. Thankfully, the letter had already been written. He had it memorized. He put pen to paper and wrote:

In that catacomb, one skull stood out from thousands...

BIKING WITH KAIJU

I RELEASE MY BIKE FROM THE DARKNESS OF THE SHED AND climb onto the cool seat, soaking in the new spring sun for a moment before I start pedaling. My skin is electric with joy as I maneuver around the last melting mounds of dirty snow and find my pace. Few things invigorate me like the first ride of the year.

Today will be good. All my hurts are still here, and I will tend to them as needed, but I am alive and I am happy. I'm going to glow for every single customer at the Co-op. I'm going to share what I'm feeling, somehow, as I scan and bag granola and veggie burgers and applesauce. And when I'm done, I'm going to ride home slow. I'm going to take the long way and breathe in blue sky. I'm going to call Bess and Stevie and Kyle and they're going to come over. We're going to drink cheap wine and watch giant monster movies on my laptop out on the porch.

Winter got rough, as it does. We fell out of the kaiju night habit, but tonight's the night to get back into it, and it's going to be all Mothra, all night. There will be arguments about this. Wine will spill as everyone talks at once. "Gamera is for the kids!" Stevie will shout over and over like a mantra. Bess will flash her sloppy calf tattoo of King Caesar drinking a smoothie, acknowledging that he kinda looks like the Cheetos cat for some reason. Kyle will get all deep -cuts ranting about Pulgasaari and the evils of capitalism. It will be great, but none of it will change the fact that Mothra is still the best kaiju forever and ever.

I coast into the co-op parking lot and don't even have to use my brakes. I just roll right to the bike rack and hop off as my front tire slides between the bars.

TAKING off my backpack to pull out my lock and chain, I notice a man standing behind me. He's a little older, early thirties maybe. "Hey," he says, in that way that guys do when they have much more to say than "Hey."

I kneel down to lock up my bike. The thing is, all the other kaiju were bad. Not Mothra. In the original movie, she caused some destruction, but only because her friends had been kidnapped. There was no maliciousness, no pointless, wanton destruction like Godzilla or any of the others delivered.

I stand and the man is still there, closer now. "Oh, I thought you were a girl."

I move past him. When Mothra first fought Godzilla, she lost. It was brutal. But her children, the larvae of Mothras-to-be, took him down. They spit their cocoon webs all over him and stopped him from destroying Tokyo.

The man follows me. "Why are you dressed like a girl?"

In the 90s Mothra movies, she destroys Ghidorah, the three-headed monster. The battles are arduous. After the stress, she regenerates. She keeps changing the colors and patterns of her wings. I can't decide which version is the prettiest. I've been watching Mothra movies all my life, but it wasn't until I saw the more recent ones that I realized that, despite her name, Mothra is not actually a moth.

She's a butterfly.

"You're a tranny, aren't you?"

Mothra is the best kaiju. She will always be the best kaiju. I refuse to concede that, no matter what anyone says.

"Fuck you, tranny!"

Mothra is beautiful.

"You're a man!"

Mothra is strong.

"You'll always be a man!"

Mothra is hope.

PIZZA_GAL_666

FIRST DATE

ONE MONTH OF ONLINE DATING AND SARAH HAD ALREADY received so many "Hey"s from BigFordChad and Smiley_Guy82 and HoneyCookie420 that Pizza_Gal_666's opener of "What's your favorite pizza?" seemed absolutely thoughtful.

"Pepperoni and sausage," Sarah messaged back.

She didn't ask Pizza_Gal_666's favorite, because her profile listed her top 25, broken down by toppings, crust type and regional style. Most were New York style, which made sense, but one was Louisville style, which Sarah was like *huh?* about.

Pizza Gal replied, "I like a girl who likes her meat lol. Wanna grab a slice?"

Sarah agreed.

That evening, she met Pizza Gal outside a new pizzeria in Williamsburg. It was opening night and the line went around the block. Sarah hovered awkwardly at the back, staring at her phone, hoping not to see the usual "Sorry, can't make it after all," but also kinda wishing for the relief from anxiety that message would bring.

Instead, she heard the clacking of high heels on blacktop and the honking of horns. Pizza Gal ran toward her through traffic in stilettos and a tight black dress with a mesh top. Her outfit had a 5-star-restaurant vibe, but also a dancing-at-the-club vibe. Definitely not a grabbing-a-slice vibe, which Sarah thought she had nailed with her Chucks, jeans and sleeveless band shirt.

Pizza Gal led with a hug, knocking Sarah's phone out of her hand in the process. Gracefully, Pizza Gal snatched it up off the sidewalk and slipped it into Sarah's back pocket even as cars still honked at her audacity.

"I'm Vannie."

"Vannie?"

"Yeah! Short for Vanessa."

"Oh! I'm Sarah."

"Thank you for showing up. So many people on that site are flakes."

"Tell me about it. I've got like a 50/50 success rate. I'm starting to get into eating out alone."

Vannie grabbed Sarah's hand for a moment. "Not too into it, I hope?" Releasing it, she added, "You are super pretty. Oh god, your skin is flawless. Your pictures don't do you justice."

Sarah reached up to cover the trio of pimples along her right jawbone. "Yeah, my camera is terrible."

"Well, should we get in line?"

"Oh, you are super pretty too!" Sarah said, hoping it wasn't too awkwardly late to return Vannie's compliment.

"Ugh, thank you. My eyeliner turned out gross."

Sarah squinted to see what was gross about the perfectly symmetrical black wings of liquid liner. "I think we're already in line actually."

Vannie looked around. "I guess we are!"

"A thousand pizza joints in this city, but this place plops a donut on a slice and puts Ataris at tables and every denim jacket owner in Williamsburg shows up."

"Does it matter why people came if the end result is the same? This energy is palpable. Can't you feel it?" Vannie closed her eyes and spread her arms, as if actually drawing in energy from all the gathered pizza eaters.

"I'm sorry." Sarah stepped back. "I was just making a joke."

"No you weren't. You were doing the whole reactionary anti-hipster thing. As if people getting together and liking a fun new thing is somehow bad? Because why? Because it's not really about the pizza for these people? Because they just want to be part of this? This excitement? This energy?"

Sarah pulled her phone out, wanting to hide in it. Before she could get it up to her face, Vannie grabbed it and slid it into her back pocket again.

"Besides," Vannie continued, "maybe I picked this place on purpose hoping there would be a line because I wanted to spend more time with you."

Sarah wondered if Vannie was just going to keep saying one perfect thing after the next, because that put a lot of pressure on her. The best she could come up with now was, "How did you find out about this place?"

Vannie shrugged. "Pizza grapevine."

"You are way into pizza."

"What are you into?"

"I like to run alone." Sarah clenched her teeth. Out of all the responses, this was the one that came out. And why did she emphasize "alone"? As opposed to running in a pack like a wolf or something?

She was getting nervous. She hadn't felt this kind of nervous in a while. Usually her dates didn't make her nervous. There was just nothing there to screw up most of the time, so it didn't matter if she said dumb things. But looking at Vannie, she wasn't sure she was ready to screw this up yet.

"Well, it pays off. You really do look amazing."

"Thanks."

"What's that T-shirt all about? Is that supposed to be a snowball?"

"It's a marshmallow. This band, they have a song about roasting marshmallows and how when one falls into the fire it's this little tragedy. I'm not really explaining it right. It's a beautiful song."

"Cool. I'd love to hear it."

"I have it on my phone actually." Sarah reached into her back pocket again. Vannie slid the phone back in, this time before it had even made it all the way out.

"I don't think this is the way I should hear it the first time, okay?"

"Oh, right."

The restaurant looked like an over-filled aquarium—high tops with people standing shoulder to shoulder around them, touching butts with people at adjacent tables. Vannie said, "It is packed, though. I hope it's not too loud to talk. Have you thought about what you want? I don't know if they do sausage and pepperoni."

"Might as well see what the hype is all about and get the donut slice."

"It's a savory donut, you know?"

"Oh."

"A blueberry donut on pizza would be gross, right?" Vannie stuck out her tongue trying to look grossed out, but ended up just looking cute. "It's a basil donut."

"Are you gonna try it?"

"Fuck yes, I am!"

"Haha. Me too then."

They eventually made it through the door. The heat from the ovens and the tightly packed bodies made Sarah sweat immediately. They were still fifteen people away from the counter when Vannie turned to her and whispered, "Oh shit. There are some people here who I, ummm, used to hang out with."

Sarah glanced around, seeing if she could guess which ones. The place was a Where's Waldo of Williamsburg hipsters, with a table full of very obvious exceptions. She giggled and pointed at it. "The ones in black cloaks?"

"They're a big deal in certain circles."

"Circles of people who wear black cloaks?"

"Yes." Vannie grabbed Sarah by the hand and pulled her out of the restaurant, knocking several baffled hipsters aside in the process.

Still giggling, Sarah argued, "But the savory donut pizza!"

Outside, they turned in one direction, only to see more of the uniquely garmented individuals walking toward them.

"Shit!" Vannie pulled Sarah the other way. "Did they see me?"

"Uh, they had the hoods of their cloaks pulled pretty low, I guess."

They ran, Vannie in her clacking black heels and Sarah in her much stealthier Chucks. Of course those people had seen Vannie. How could anyone not see Vannie? Sarah thought she had even seen them nod at her.

"Are you up for a subway ride? I know a perfect place next to Coney Island."

"That's a long trip," Sara said.

"They serve legit New York slices, not this hipster shit."

"Oh, so now it's hipster shit?"

"Who puts donuts on pizza?"

"Fucking hipsters!"

They didn't stop running until they were on the L-train, out of breath but still laughing.

Sarah asked, "The people in cloaks. That was weird, right?"

Vannie shrugged.

"Or is that the new hipster thing? Like, denim is out, cloaks are in?"

Vannie looked her in the eyes and held both of Sarah's hands. "I'm sorry, but you need to take them seriously. They are powerful. They can make people do things."

"I…" Sarah said as Vannie squeezed her hands tighter. "Okay?"

Sarah decided not to talk about the cloak people. It was probably some hipster Goth thing. She'd seen weirder. Vannie didn't seem Goth, but she was wearing all black. Maybe she was in Goth recovery.

They held hands all the way to the pizza joint, a block from Coney Island, on an otherwise dark and empty stretch of road. It was just a window in a brick facade, staffed by an old sweaty guy with a classic Brooklyn accent.

"The usual?" he asked.

"Of course."

Twenty minutes later, he slid a box through the window without Sarah even seeing money change hands. They carried it to the beach, out onto the pier..

Sitting cross-legged, they faced each other. Vannie's dress was hiked up to show a lot of leg and a sliver of black panties that Sarah only glanced at. They placed the pizza box on their feet and flipped the lid open, releasing a puff of steam into the New York night. "The usual" was a piping hot pie with mushrooms and onions, sliced into a bizarre pattern. Sarah didn't even get how the pattern was possible, with all the curves and angles. It would have taken a very skilled hand with a pizza cutter.

"Oh! I'm used to triangle slices." Fingertip above the sizzling cheese, Sarah traced the various half moons and complex vertices. "Why this?"

"For protection," Vannie replied before taking a bite.

"Don't burn yourself!"

"It's fine! Try it!"

Sarah picked up an oddly shaped slice and tentatively took a bite. To her surprise, it was the perfect temperature. And it was delicious.

They ate a few more slices in smiling silence, greasy fingers catching the moonlight, as the ocean whooshed gently over the shore nearby.

After eating far more slices than someone her size should be able to hold, Vannie leaned back slightly, rubbing her tummy through her black dress. She moved forward and put her face close to Sarah's. Sarah held her breath as Vannie slipped her hand into Sarah's back pocket and took out her phone.

"Now would be the perfect time to play me your T-shirt song."

SECOND DATE

As Sarah hit her stride, her cellphone vibrated in her armband. She groaned half-heartedly, as if she hadn't intentionally accidentally forgot to turn it off for her run like usual, as if she wasn't ecstatic that it might be another text from Vannie.

When she saw that it was her mom instead, she groaned for real. Another random "I'm proud of you" text, to which she resisted the urge to reply, "For what, Mom? Quitting school or working in a running-shoe store?" Sometimes Sarah got the impression that her mother was just pleased to know her daughter was alive and making her way in the world and expected nothing more from her. Maybe that was true. Or maybe her mom harbored some secret disappointment that she wasn't a lawyer or didn't have a boyfriend or didn't eat broccoli. That's what moms did, right? They weren't just happy their kids were breathing.

Jogging in place, she looked back at an exchange with

Vannie from earlier that week, a couple days after their date. Vannie had sent a quote from the song, the perfect quote, and a heart. Okay, three hearts. And three hearts meant something. She didn't know what, exactly, but definitely something. Unfortunately, Sarah had replied with the next line of the song, "That chocolate will never know the life it could have had," and five hearts. The absolute dumbness of it still made her feel like she had sucked cinder blocks into her stomach. But Vannie had come back with "LOL I am so happy I found you on that site! When is our second date?" so it couldn't have been too dumb.

They had made plans for tonight, and Sarah wished she could run through time right up to the point at which she was supposed to meet Vannie, but she couldn't. Instead, she ran as fast as she could through Prospect Park, hoping to make her legs look extra toned, because she was going to wear a dress this time.

That night, Sarah met Vannie at a vegetarian pizza place in the East Village. They got two slices each and walked around talking so much that their second slices got cold before they made it through their first.

"We could throw them away," Sarah suggested.

"Fuck you!"

"Why did we even get two slices?"

"Because who eats just one slice of pizza?"

"I guess."

"Let's go to my place. I have a microwave."

"Okay, yeah."

They took the train back to Vannie's apartment. Walking up the steps of a pristine brownstone on a well-manicured street lined with expensive cars, Sarah said, "Holy shit, you must have like 700 roommates to afford this place!"

"I live alone actually."

Stunned, Sarah followed Vannie inside and gasped. It was unreal, a TV apartment. Sarah, along with most of her friends, even the ones with a decent job or two, had room-mates and at least one piece of furniture salvaged from a dumpster. Not Vannie. Everything was pristine, from the spot-less white leather couch to the coffee table that might have been made out of rare gems to the framed portraits of pizzas on the walls, each cut into arcane shapes. Okay, that was weird, but still sorta classy. Who the fuck was this girl?

"What do you do again? For work?"

Vannie rolled her eyes. "I'm independently wealthy."

"Uh-huh."

Sarah wasn't one hundred percent sure Vannie was kidding. If she was, she obviously didn't want to say what she did for real. If she wasn't, she didn't seem interested in elabo-rating on the source of her wealth.

So Sarah joked, "From some pizza related endeavor?"

"Of course," Vannie replied, following Sarah as she nosed around the place. In the kitchen, Sarah found an array of pizza cutters hung on pegboard on the wall like tools in a construction worker's home shop. Their blades gleamed.

Sarah took one down. It looked old somehow, even though it was so shiny. The patterns carved into the handle were similar to those in the pizzas they'd eaten together, and those framed on the wall.

"Seriously though, what's with that design? Owww!" She dropped the utensil on the floor. Blood dripped onto the white tile around it from a fresh cut on her opposite hand. She looked at it in disbelief. Had she just cut herself? She couldn't remember rolling the blade against her palm, but she must have.

Unfazed, Vannie grabbed a towel from a drawer.

"It's… It's sharp," Sarah said, still shocked.

"What good is a dull blade? Here…" Vannie pressed the towel against Sarah's palm, soaking up most of the blood. Then she pulled Sarah's hand up to her face. For a moment, Sarah thought Vannie was going to lick the wound, but she didn't. "It's not bad. No need for stitches or anything."

"I can't believe I did that."

"Sometimes our bodies are compelled to do things our minds don't agree to."

"What?"

Vannie led Sarah by her uncut hand to a spacious bathroom. Sarah usually only saw bathrooms so well-lit on the rare occasion she stayed at a nice-ish hotel on one of her running road trips. Vannie sat her down on the edge of the tub, kneeled in front of her and carefully washed and bandaged the wound.

"Thank you," Sarah said.

"Did you get any blood on your dress?"

"Oh fuck!" Sarah panicked. She jumped up and inspected her dress in the mirror. Thankfully, she didn't see any bloodstains. "I don't think so."

"Good. That dress is gorgeous."

Sarah sat back down on the ledge of the tub and Vannie squeezed in beside her. Vannie kissed her lightly on the cheek. "I think we get along well."

Giggling at the unromantic and uncharacteristically awkward statement, Sarah agreed and upped the ante. "Fuck it, I like you."

They touched lips, almost too briefly to even call it a kiss. Then they pulled apart, smiling. Sarah put her fingertips over her mouth as if to stop it from going back for more, even though she wanted to. And why shouldn't she? This felt good. They did get along well, like really well.

"I want to see the rest of this shit hole. You have more than a kitchen and bathroom, right?"

Sarah poked around, playfully opening closet doors, but not really looking inside. She just didn't want to run straight to the bedroom.

"Does your hand hurt?" Vannie asked, following Sarah.

Sarah opened a media cabinet next to the flatscreen in the living room and scanned the DVD titles. "What the fuck? This is all '90s gross-out comedies?"

Vannie shrugged.

"I wish I hadn't seen this." Sarah closed the cabinet. She stood and turned around. Smirking, she maneuvered past Vannie and proceeded toward the last room, the bedroom.

She fingered the wall inside the door and found the light switch. Flicking it on, she braced herself, half expecting to see a cheese-colored bedspread with pepperoni pillows. Instead, she was pleasantly surprised to find tasteful, pale pink sheets on a queen-sized bed. She plopped down on it.

Then she noticed the black cloak hanging from a hook behind the door.

"So your old friends…?"

Vannie frowned. "They're…"

"A group of cloak aficionados who really like eating pizza?"

"It's not just about eating pizza," Vannie replied, almost angrily.

"What, do they worship pizza? Is it a pizza cult? Do they chant sacred pizza chants and carve arcane symbols into their… Oh. Holy shit. Pizza Gal 666. I thought the 666 was a joke, like how everyone says they're a witch now but mainly they just like eyeliner and scented candles."

"It's not like that."

"You were in this cult?"

"You need to stop talking about this actually. We can… They can bend people, remap the now, carving unwanted futures into our timelines."

Sarah stared at the floor, so lost for words she was trying to divine the chaotic patterns of the carpet fibers around her feet in hopes they might tell her what to do next. On the one hand, she liked Vannie. The thought of her already filled Sarah's head with visions of late-night smooches and hand-in-hand vacations to ancient ruins and all the future stuff she thought about when smitten. On the other pizza-cutter sliced hand, this was not right, and even as her gut twisted in smitten-ness, it also turned in sensing that Vannie wasn't being exactly forthright.

Sarah moved away from the bed. "I don't... Okay, I'm sorry, this is weird. I need to go. And never do online dating again."

She hurried past Vannie toward the front door. Vannie chased after her, "Don't be like this. I'm not weird. You know I'm not weird."

"Do I?"

"Okay, maybe a little weird, but not run-out-of-my-bedroom-in-fear weird!"

Vannie grabbed Sarah's hand, not in a malicious, *I'm-going-to-stop-you* sort of way, but in a *hey-it's-okay* sort of way. And Sarah did feel okay. As weird as this stuff seemed, she did not feel afraid. She did not actually feel like doing anything other than staying with this amazing woman.

"But you're done with them?"

Vannie nodded.

"If I stay, you're taking me out for Indian food next time, got it?"

Vannie bit her lip hesitantly, looking remarkably cute.

"Got it?"

"Fine!"

THIRD DATE

Despite how well their last date had ended up going once Vannie put her cloak away, and despite Vannie's reassurances, Sarah still had a nagging feeling that something was up. However, that didn't stop her head from filling so full of daydreams she felt like she was floating even as her toes propelled her across mile after mile of Brooklyn sidewalk. She fixated on the handholding. She had never been much of a hand holder, in part because the men she had dated in the past held her hand as if holding her captive. But when Vannie's palm had first touched hers, it felt electric. Now, half the time when she thought of the two of them together, she pictured their disembodied hands, each with its own heart beating in time with the other's, moving through life impervious to whatever the world might throw at them.

She caught herself in this thought and realized how mushy and teenage naïve it was. Instead of running faster to clear her head, she slowed down and reached for her phone to read old texts. In the process, she bobbled it and it bounced onto the hood of a parked car. When she picked it up, she saw a figure in a black cloak across the street. Now she did run faster.

A few hours later, she ran again, this time to catch the train for her date with Vannie. In her hurry, she tripped and nearly fell into the train, letting the momentum carry her to her seat. When she looked up, she noticed a black-cloaked figure a couple seats ahead of her, facing the opposite direction. No big deal, she told herself. Just a random person in a cloak. Nothing to do with her at all. She was almost getting used to seeing them.

When the cloaked person turned around, face enshadowed so that only a cheese-stained scowl showed through, Sarah sank into her seat.

Getting off a stop early, she speed-walked to Mysore Feast, where Vannie was supposed to meet her. She felt certain Vannie wasn't going to show up. Even though she had promised, Sarah was convinced she wouldn't eat anything but pizza. She wished she had dug around more in Vannie's kitchen. Maybe she would have found cupboards full of ramen and cereal to dispel the crazy idea that Vannie was a… pizzavore. *Next time*, she told herself. If there was a next time.

Sarah was surprised to see Vannie standing outside the

restaurant, in heels as usual. She was holding a hand to her stomach though, and, as Sarah got closer, she could see that Vannie didn't look happy.

"Are you okay?" Sarah asked as they hugged.

"Just a stomach thing."

"I'm sorry. Do you want to postpone? You could have called."

"I wanted to see you."

"I wanted to see you too!"

They kissed gently, keeping eye contact as their lips touched. As they pulled apart, Vannie said, "Indian might be too spicy for my tum tonight, though. Could we go someplace else?"

Sarah's heart sank. "Yeah, sure."

"I know a place around the block that has killer pies." Vannie brightened.

"You don't think pizza would be too hard on your stomach?"

"Pizza? What's hard on the stomach about pizza?"

"I guess I don't know. I mean, we could, like, do soup or something?"

"You want to take me out for soup?"

"Or something?"

"You are so fucking cute. I am infinitely glad I found you." She snatched Sarah's hand. "Now come on! Pizza ahoy!"

Sarah walked slowly, dreading the pizza place. "So, I've been seeing a lot of people in black cloaks lately."

"Seeing or noticing?"

"Huh?"

"Seeing them or noticing them? Like, you probably saw them before, but you didn't notice them until now that you know about them. It's like when you learn a new word and suddenly start hearing it everywhere."

"I'm pretty sure I would have noticed people in black

cloaks if I saw them before. And I'm pretty sure they're following me."

Vannie stopped suddenly. "What? Why would you think that?"

"Like, the one I saw on the way here, they looked at me."

"Looked at you, or in your direction?"

"I couldn't tell because of the hood."

"Why would they follow you?"

"I don't know. If they, like, think I'm taking you away from them… I don't know. It just seems weird."

"You're being paranoid."

"When you said they could make people do things?"

"Apparently they can make you leave me!" Vannie shouted, startling Sarah, not just because of the abruptness, but because she hadn't really thought that—not even three dates in—they had established the sort of relationship wherein Sarah bowing out constituted "leaving me."

"I'm not leaving you," Sarah whispered, unconvinced.

"Good. Can we get pizza now?"

"Yeah."

They walked the rest of the way in silence, holding hands. Sarah kept her grip loose. She didn't want to slide her hand away, but if Vannie let go she wouldn't mind.

At the pizza place, they found a corner table. Sarah sat with her back against the wall, perusing the menu as the waitress formally welcomed Vannie back, perhaps too formally for a random former member of the black cloak club. The thought crossed Sarah's mind, what if Vannie was still in this cult? And what if she was more than just a regular member?

When the waitress left, Vannie said, "I love this place so much."

"Oh, what a surprise."

When she realized her comment may have come off a bit more cutting than she intended, she pulled her face out of the menu and smiled at her date. Vannie was pretty. How a girl who ate so much pizza could look so pristine was beyond Sarah's comprehension. And she liked Sarah, and vice versa. They were three dates in. How long had it been since she had made it three dates with someone she liked this much?

"There's an artichoke pie that is absolutely killer," Vannie said.

Sarah started to respond but stopped when she noticed half a dozen cloaked people scattered through the restaurant. Their hoods were all aimed her way.

She leaned closer to Vannie. "They're here."

"Of course they are. It's a pizza place."

"How can you be so casual about this?"

"It's pizza. It's casual dining."

"I mean, about your former weird… friends… following us around. Last time you saw them, we ran away, remember?"

Vannie reached out to straighten the shakers of parmesan and red pepper flakes. She made a waving gesture in the process. It was subtle, but Sarah noticed it, and so did the black cloaks. Suddenly, they all held their menus in front of their faces. Vannie had signaled them, and they had responded, puppets at her command.

"Let's just enjoy some delicious pizza," Vannie said.

"You know, let's not." Sarah pushed her chair back and it scraped loudly against the floor. As if choreographed, all menus dropped at the same time and the enshadowed faces behind them turned toward her. "Let's go someplace else."

"I need pizza."

"No, you don't."

"I do."

A voice in Sarah's head was shouting: *She is pretty and rich and smart and she likes you* so loud Sarah could hardly hear her own voice as she said, "I think your life is too complicated for me right now, so I'm going to get some takeout from the Indian place and head home."

Sarah paused, waiting for Vannie to come to her senses and flee beside her. Instead, the waitress arrived with another oddly cut pizza they hadn't even ordered.

Vannie's voice turned hard as she looked up from the pie at Sarah. "Do not fucking leave me."

Sarah flipped the pizza onto the floor, stepped over the steaming mess, and left.

SARAH WALKED FAST, but not too fast to delete every text from Vannie along the way. As she did, she read them again. Teardrops plopped onto the screen, blurring the words. She hated crying over this stupid girl she had only seen three times. But fuck, pizza notwithstanding, they had been good times. Whatever. She'd just have to move on to BigFordChad or some other boring jerk.

When she entered the subway, the station was shoulder-to-shoulder with people in black cloaks. Sarah wasn't even surprised. She tried not to look at them, but she felt their eyes on her. Why did they care now? She had made enough of a scene that they had to know she was no longer encroaching on their territory. That wasn't it though, was it? That had never been why they were following her.

She didn't want to think Vannie was a part of this, wanted to take the woman at her word. But she had seen the wave in the restaurant, small as it was. She had seen the black cloaks' response. And she knew Vannie had waved them on now too.

Sarah toed the yellow line. Turning to the woman next to her, she asked, "Aren't you creeped out by these people in black cloaks?"

"What? Uh-uh, I ain't dealing with no crazies today!" The woman stormed off.

The black cloaks tightened around Sarah, inhaling all the

air on the platform taking it away from her. A man cut through them casually and stood next to her to wait for the train. He was an older guy in a wardrobe that indicated he might be homeless or work at a really cool record store.

"Hey, excuse me," she said loudly as the sound of the approaching train filled the station. "Do you see the people in black cloaks?"

The man's eyes went wide as he gazed around, suddenly upset. She held up her hands, trying to calm him. Seeing the cut on her palm made him even crazier. She looked at the wound, the blackened scabs now formed a familiar pattern.

The man moved to the edge of the platform. "Nonononono…"

The shrill sound of wheels scraping rails buried his wild cries.

He took one more glance back and then leapt onto the tracks just as the train arrived. It did not stop. When it passed, she looked down between the scratched silver rails to see a smear of meat and blood that looked for all the world like a…

She spun around, but the black cloaks were gone now. The crowd backed away from her, trembling with fear. A police officer broke through, and a woman- the woman Sarah had spoken with earlier-grabbed the officer by the sleeve. She pointed at Sarah. "That crazy bitch threw that man in front of the train."

The crowd shouted in agreement.

"I saw it."

"She did it."

"She killed him."

Sarah turned to leave, but there was nowhere to go.

Shaking, she looked down at her scarred hand as the rats began their hungry work on the mess on the tracks.

PREVIOUS APPEARANCES

- "Animal Behavior" first appeared in Rosalind's Siblings: Fiction and Poetry Celebrating Scientists of Marginalized Genders
- "Five Ways to Kill Your Rapist on a Farm" first appeared in Dark Matter Presents Human Monsters: A Horror Anthology
- "Necksnapper" first appeared in The Dark #31
- "The Songwriter's Fingers" first appeared in Revolver, reprinted in Berzerkoids
- "Feed My Corpse to Sharks" first appeared in Berzerkoids
- "Rolled Up" first appeared in Zombie Punks Fuck Off
- "Huntress" is original to this collection
- "A Centauress Walks Into a Battle" first appeared in Forbidden Futures #4
- "Drowner" first appeared in Every Day Fiction
- "Love Skull" first appeared in Dark Discoveries #33
- "Biking With Kaiju" first appeared in The Forge
- "Pizza_Gal_666" first appeared in Tales from the Crust: an Anthology of Pizza Horror

ABOUT THE AUTHOR

Emma Alice Johnson grows wildflowers and writes. She lives on a farm dedicated to conservation of native plants and endangered insects. She has released many zines and books for adults and children, with subject matter ranging from nature to pop culture to horror. When she isn't planting or writing, she can be found running through the woods with her pet pig, singing to her chickens, lifting weights, watching B-movies or reading while snuggled with her cat. Learn more at www.freaktension.com

ALSO FROM WEIRDPUNK BOOKS

Profane Altars: Weird Sword & Sorcery - edited by Sam Richard

In the spirit of Robert E. Howard, Tanith Lee, Karl Edward Wagner, and films like *Conquest* and *Fire & Ice* comes *Profane Altars: Weird Sword and Sorcery*. Underground horror authors Emma Alice Johnson, Matthew Mitchell, Adam Smith, Sara Century, Charles Austin Muir, Edwin Callihan, and editor Sam Richard conjure forth visions of the unknowable and ancient past.

Featuring cover art by the legendary Jeffrey Catherine Jones.

Infinity Mathing at the Shore & Other Disruptions - M. Lopes da Silva

A heartfelt, disquieting collection of short stories focused on body horror, transness, anti-capitalism, queerness, decay, transformation, living buildings, rot, ruin, vintage arcade games, and so much more. With *Infinity Mathing at the Shore & Other Disruptions*, M. Lopes da Silva has solidified themself as an essential and sharp voice in the canon of 21st century queer horror.

Cover art by legendary punk artist Croad.

Feral Architecture: Ballardian Horrors - edited by Sam Richard

J.G. Ballard has held a tremendous influence on culture since he first started writing, much of which turned out to be prophetic. In *Feral Architecture* Joe Koch, Donyae Coles, Sara Century, Brendan Vidito, and editor Sam Richard plume the depth of that influence through the lens of horror fiction.

The results are surreal, ominous, unexpected, unnerving, and a fitting tribute to the legacy of one of the 20th century's most impactful and important writers.

Featuring a foreword by Scott Dwyer of The Plutonian.

Thank you for picking up this Weirdpunk book!
We're a small press out of Minneapolis, MN and our goal is to publish interesting and unique titles in all varieties of weird horror and splatterpunk, often from queer writers. It is our hope that if you like one of our releases, you will like the others.
If you enjoyed this book, please check out what else we have to offer, drop a review, and tell your friends about us.
Buying directly from us is the best way to support what we do.
www.weirdpunkbooks.com

Printed in the USA
CPSIA information can be obtained
at www.ICGtesting.com
JSHW081438171024
71731JS00002B/10